AMUN

A GATHERING OF INDIGENOUS STORIES

AMUN

A GATHERING OF INDIGENOUS STORIES

Natasha Kanapé Fontaine ~ Melissa Mollen Dupuis ~ Louis-Karl Picard-Sioui
Virginia Pésémapéo Bordeleau ~ Naomi Fontaine ~ Alyssa Jérôme ~ Michel Jean
Jean Sioui ~ Maya Cousineau-Mollen ~ Joséphine Bacon

SELECTED BY

Michel Jean

TRANSLATED BY

Kathryn Gabinet-Kroo

EXILE
editions

singular fiction, poetry, nonfiction, translation, drama, and graphic books

Library and Archives Canada Cataloguing in Publication

Title: Amun : a gathering of Indigenous stories / Natasha Kanapé Fontaine,
Melissa Mollen Dupuis, Louis-Karl Picard-Sioui, Virginia Pésémapéo Bordeleau,
Naomi Fontaine, Alyssa Jérôme, Michel Jean, Jean Sioui, Maya Cousineau-
Mollen, Joséphine Bacon ; selected by Michel Jean ; translated by Kathryn
Gabinet-Kroo.
Other titles: Amun. English
Names: Jean, Michel, 1960- editor. | Gabinet-Kroo, Kathryn, 1953- translator.
Description: Translation of: Amun : nouvelles.
Identifiers: Canadiana (print) 20200199056 | Canadiana (ebook) 20200199110 |
ISBN 9781550968774 (softcover) | ISBN 9781550968781 (EPUB) |
ISBN 9781550968798 (Kindle) | ISBN 9781550968804 (PDF)
Subjects: LCSH: Short stories, Canadian. | CSH: Canadian literature—Native
authors. | LCGFT: Short stories.
Classification: LCC PS8235.I6 A4813 2020 | DDC C843/.0108897—dc23

Original title: AMUN. Copyright © Les Éditions Internationales Alain Stanké,
Montréal, Canada, 2016. All rights reserved
Translation copyright © Kathryn Gabinet-Kroo, 2020
Cover woodcut by Jef Thompson
Book designed by Michael Callaghan
Typeset in Fairfield and Plantagenet Cherokee fonts at Moons of Jupiter Studios
Published by Exile Editions Ltd ~ www.ExileEditions.com
144483 Southgate Road 14 – GD, Holstein, Ontario, N0G 2A0
Printed and Bound in Canada by Marquis

We gratefully acknowledge the Canada Council for the Arts, the Government of Canada,
the Ontario Arts Council, and the Ontario Media Development Corporation for their
support toward our publishing activities.

Conseil des Arts   Canada Council
du Canada   for the Arts

Canada

ONTARIO ARTS COUNCIL
CONSEIL DES ARTS DE L'ONTARIO
an Ontario government agency
un organisme du gouvernement de l'Ontario

Ontario
Ontario Media Development
Corporation

Canadian sales representation: The Canadian Manda Group, 664 Annette Street,
Toronto ON M6S 2C8 www.mandagroup.com 416 516 0911

North American and international distribution, and U.S. sales:
Independent Publishers Group, 814 North Franklin Street,
Chicago IL 60610 www.ipgbook.com toll free: 1 800 888 4741

ix | *Introduction*
   Michel Jean

1 | *I Burned All the Letters in My First Name*
   Natasha Kanapé Fontaine

8 | *Memekueshu*
   Melissa Mollen Dupuis

25 | *Hannibalo-God-Mozilla Against the Great Cosmic Void*
   Louis-Karl Picard-Sioui

37 | *The Lakota Shaman*
   Virginia Pésémapéo Bordeleau

45 | *Neka*
   Naomi Fontaine

52 | *Snowy Owl*
   Alyssa Jérôme

58 | *Where Are You?*
   Michel Jean

72 | *The Tomahawk Strikes a Blow*
   Jean Sioui

78 | *Mitatamun Means Regret*
   Maya Cousineau-Mollen

93 | *Nashtash in the Big City*
   Joséphine Bacon

97 | *The Authors*

101 | *Translator's Note*

INTRODUCTION

In the past, life was simpler. The world's rules, which had been set well before we arrived, enabled us to lead a life that was both humble and harsh. A life dictated by our surroundings.

Those who lived in the forest hunted for that which it housed – birds, beasts, fish – and gathered berries, plants, and their roots. Those whose territory covered the plains tracked the immense and endless herds. The nations settled near the ocean lived off it; from the South to the Far North, it fed them.

Some people tend to idealize the past, but it was not a perfect world. There were territorial disputes, Innu against Inuit, wars, Mohawks against Wendats, and so on. We were only human, shaped by wants, needs, desires and dreams.

Today, we often hold onto the image of a world fixed in time and space while modern societies are seen evolving. It was, however, a world in perpetual motion.

Thus, my family, the Pekuakamiulnuatsh (Innu from Mashteuiatsh), like other Innu, lived according to nature's rhythm. The clans spent the summer on the banks of the Pekuakami, which served as an assembly point.

Summer was an easy season. The game was varied and the weather mild. For the Innu, it was vacation time, in a certain sense, and it ended with the onset of autumn when the whole community prepared to leave for the hunting grounds. Each family had its own.

The lands of the Siméon clan, to which I belong and which was called Atuk (Caribou) before white priests arrived with their Bibles and facilitated the appropriation of territory and colonization, were found in a place known as Passes-Dangereuses. To get there, the family had to leave Mashteuiatsh in mid-August and first skirt the lake to the mouth of the Peribonka River, then take the long, arduous trail upstream to reach the river's source.

This was a fast-flowing river with many rapids that canoes could not navigate, so they were portaged and steep mountains were scaled to avoid the rushing water. Everyone carried their load, young and old alike.

When we got to Passes-Dangereuses, we set up camp in anticipation of winter, and the whole family participated. We were home. It was our territory and we were proud of it.

Finding food in the forest was daily work to which everyone contributed. The men tracked big game far to the north. The women set traps for hares, hunted partridge around the encampment. We called that *petite chasse* or small-game hunting. The women also maintained the tents and cared for the children.

With the first warmth of spring, all the Pekuakamiulnuatsh were happy to go back down to the Pekuakami. This trip required careful preparation, leaving behind what could be left, bringing the minimum but taking the skins, of course. The sale of the haul from a winter of hunting and trapping would finance the next trip back to our territory.

In early June, the families finally returned to the sandy shores of Mashteuiatsh. The circle was complete. A year had passed. After months of living in isolation, this was reunion time for everyone. It was Amun: the time of gathering.

Life required families to travel great distances. They never stopped for long, living as nomads did. The Innu called this world Nitassinan. The Cree called it Eeyou Istchee, the Abenaki called it Ndakinna, and the Wendat, Nionwentsïo, and so on. They weren't perfect worlds. But they were ours.

Today, life is not so simple. Our territories are occupied, exploited. The forest has become a resource, the rivers too, the same goes for the fish and the game. The meaning of things has changed.

We live on reserves that were once our summer gathering places and we no longer leave them. Those who do, live in the city. Through marriage, they gradually merge with the Whites, like a fistful of red earth thrown onto the pale sand on a beach.

We have survived throughout the millennia according to rules that we had accepted. And in a few generations, we had to change our life. It was not easy and it created a lot of pain. Now we live differently.

But the spirit of long ago was never extinguished. The lands are still there. And a better world lives in our hearts.

The book that you are about to read is a gathering. As it used to be, when we all left for our lands to rejoin our people at the agreed upon place. Amun.

Michel Jean

I BURNED ALL THE LETTERS IN MY FIRST NAME

Natasha Kanapé Fontaine
Innu from Pessamit

No, I don't know how to do throat singing. I'm not Inuk. I wouldn't want to disrespect their tradition. No, I don't know how to do beats. Like her. No, I don't know how to play an instrument, like you. No, I don't know how to play the guitar, the drum, the flute, whatever. I'm not at all what you want most in the world to hold in your loving arms at night.

I didn't come here to end up in the arms of a pop singer only to be dumped for a throat singer. I may not be from your tribe, but that doesn't mean I'm not extraordinary. I do know how to play with my native tongue. I love to read poetry out loud. But I know that's not often done around here.

Another day to get through. It's been five days since you told me you're going back to your ex. I didn't cry. I just know that, since that time, the winds have kicked up outside. I hear them at night. They'd say that's why I don't sleep at night. I don't know. Sometimes it calms me down, and sometimes it keeps me up.

So no, I haven't found the right guy yet. The quintessential "native" – long hair, bracelets beaded by his mother, moccasins waiting for him on the doorstep at home. An Innu, Mohawk, whatever you like. But no. I tend to think that the guys back home have a fondness for the bottle. It depends on their parents. But the good ones are all taken if they're not married yet. And the best-looking ones are all paired up. You just have to know how to catch them when they're between girlfriends. Then again, they prefer the ones who already have kids, or so it seems. Our boys all need love and sometimes the best way to get it is to give it, even when you haven't any left.

I love our guys anyway. They aren't mean-spirited, except when they're intoxicated. It depends whether they're drunk or drugged. But I don't go to that kind of party. And I've heard it's much worse in other places. The fact remains that six years ago my cousin went to prison for murdering his girlfriend. He loved that girl to pieces. They were one of the most beautiful couples on the reserve. And then he killed her. But it was because of the mescaline.

After all, it's not true that they are, at heart, unkind. As I see it, our boys are the handsomest and the sweetest. Never dishonest. It's the need, the deprivation, and the poverty that breed nastiness, when you have no pride to begin with. Whenever someone acts superior, everyone laughs at him. That's the way it is. You have no right to act like you're better than everyone else. Nor do you have the right to act like you're any worse.

It just goes to show that you still have to pay attention sometimes. I often wonder whether you were on something, that first time you came over. I wonder. But that was a year ago. This year, you're different. Much more luminous. More present. With you, it doesn't bother me. It doesn't bother me that you drink, that you party like hell, that you sniff whenever and whatever you want. With me, you have the Gladue Decision, as they'd say in court. The Gladue Decision... I don't know what to make of that either. When it's not about contempt, it's all about pity. I want to say that I *see* you. I understand you. I know where you're headed. In spite of it all.

Montreal. City of Lights, as my grandfather might have said. It's already been four years since I moved here. Time flies. I've worked in cafés, sold beauty products, mopped floors. Anything to survive.

I went back to see your show the other night, in that little bar where a bunch of Inuit all pile in to see you sing. To hear you shout. To see you smile.

I'd love to be able to erase all the darkness in people's eyes. Seems to me that I'm okay, I came through it all right. But that night in the bar, I met that girl whose eyes fascinated me. I saw her with her boozed-up boyfriend, who was busy pawing her. Until we all went out to smoke, I was with my percussionist friend, the curly-haired Cuban guy that she liked so much. Her boyfriend did not like the way she looked at my friend or that she told him he had nice hair.

There's that subconscious that speaks to us on the sly: "He has nicer hair than I do, he's extraordinary. Back home we're all the same, so you'd fucking unload me for the new guy and his pretty curls. For someone better because me, I'm nobody because I'm not extraordinary. I'm not majestic."

At that point her boyfriend whispered in her ear, his eyes on fire. Brutishly and shamelessly sliding his hand over her pants and onto her pubis so that the curly-haired Cuban could clearly see that she belonged to him.

They go back in. I follow them. The guy falls to his knees in front of her. She moves forward, and he holds onto her leg. I shout, "I see you!" to tell him that they're not alone. He lets her go. She keeps moving forward, back straight, in a hurry to get back to the bar where you're singing.

Going back inside. Seeing all those people proudly dancing to a song whose lyrics I do not understand. A man approaches, apparently happy to see me. He smiles at me. I smile back. He asks if I'm Mohawk. I say no. I'm Innu.

"That's great. Nice to meet you. Nice hat." He speaks to me in English.

"Thank you so much," I reply in kind.

Despite everything, I felt incredibly alone with myself at that moment.

With you on stage.

Because I lived where Quebeckers live, among them, I've always had trouble getting close to my own people. Because I grew up in their society and learned no other codes of behaviour, I observe from a distance those who are within me and those from whom I come. Today, I am not so timid, so I have an easier time adapting to situations, to personalities, to individuals and to others.

But when I recognize the smile and the look in the eyes of any "Native," I always recognize myself. I recognize my father, I recognize my grandfather. And, in each woman I recognize my mother and my grandmother. I exist.

For a long time, I believed that we were weird. That I was marginal, eccentric. That I took up too much space. Then when I go back home to my village and finally see "natives" all over the place, I recognize myself. I was never marginal. We all have the same personality.

At last.

I didn't go back to see you sing at that little bar on Atwater. It was too hard. Even if I want you, even if I accept everything about you, I can't stretch myself wide enough to swallow all this pain. To take it all. I just can't.

I don't know how you do it. Me, I would have immediately fallen to pieces.

Maybe that's exactly the point. That you hide it so well, that you swallow it down, again and again and again.

Like a bottomless pit, we drink all that we can drink. Our infinite thirst is akin to the internal pain that is passed on through generations and centuries. You and I, together, would be a foolish combination of all those violations, all those dispossessions and all the howling screams that we both carry in our DNA. When I drink, it never ends. I never know when I fall asleep. I just keep waking up time after time. I'm sure it's the same for you.

I feel like burning all the letters of my first name. I am not Russian. I'm not English either, and even less a Quebecker. I want a name like Maïkan. People will call me "she-wolf" in my language, and I'll recognize myself immediately. My body will remind people of the elders, who could smile in their white graves.

I'll have a different personality, and it will call upon the entire earth, upon everything that was here before we came along. It is not true that I'm dreaming. It is not true that it's a legend.

I know that it is true.

Everything that's in our blood.

Our blood burns us so; that's why we think that liquor will finally put the fire out. It's like the sun burning our skin ever more each year. It's like Fort McMurray imitating the fires of hell brought to us by the missionaries. No one believes in Hades anymore, so we can no longer extinguish the flames. They're the ones who brought that notion to us. Hell was something we knew nothing about.

Because my twin flame does not recognize me, the forests are ablaze.

⁂

It's hazy. An incandescent morning. The light is getting on my nerves. I want to be given a different name, to be named for a season. Shikuan is pretty: spring. Uapukun: I could be every-one's flower. Maïkaniss: little she-wolf. She can howl any way she wants to, the better to speak to the ancestors who hide in the trees of the far-off land. Shutshiun: strength. Because I can pass through the smoke. I could call myself Strength. Uasheshkun: blue sky. Like my friend with her smile. Blue sky or a sunny spell after everything she's gone through in her life. Uasheshkun, who knows everything, who's studying philosophy. Uash, the one we love when we're drinking shooters. Uash, the one we envy because she's so beautiful. Uash, the one who walks along the streets of Montreal. An enlightening.

Evening. The bottle is there waiting for me. I'm waiting for you. I'm waiting for you to pop up on Facebook. Outside it's grey, almost foggy. I have a vision of rain. Nothing ever quenches our thirst for the other. Never. Touching you is like caressing the madness that is there, on the other side of the door. We no longer know if it's the city or the centuries that are just hanging around, as if we're going to throw ourselves into their arms. Raven. Outside. On the neighbour's balcony. It's your hair, and your eyes that sparkle in the night or when the sun comes up. As hot as the sun that rises over shoulders in the summer. Where are you, in the city? Where can I find you so that I can jump into your arms, so I can drink your thirst, so you'll stop using alcohol as an escape? I know that I love you to death, my veins are on fire. I'd like to find you in the North, but Nunavik holds too many secrets for the Innu. It's either always daytime or always night-time. It's in your eternal snow that I recognize my reflection, but no one's heard from you in a while. You left with her, with the one who finds her reflection in your eyes while I search for my face. I'd like to know that you're playing in Montreal at night, but you won't sing. But then what would I be doing there, wanting to love everyone again and breaking my heart for nothing?

We must hope that the North and the South will stop looking at each other from afar; we must burn with desire for the caribou herds to return to our lands and for the sound of their hooves going back and forth between North and South, as it was before, once again linking our luminosities above the wintry winds.

My feet, my hands and the tip of my nose froze as I waited for you. I should go back inside.

But I'm still thirsty.

⁂

Here, in the midst of the woods, I write my foreign name on a piece of bark. It looks like paper. I cast it into the fire.

MEMEKUESHU

Melissa Mollen Dupuis
Innu from Ekuanitshit

Shitty idea. Shitty idea! Unbelievably shitty idea!!

Nish had nothing but her inner monologue to keep her warm as she sat on her snowmobile. It was easy to follow the path well-defined by the vehicles that had gone before her. A twelve-member film crew tended to leave its mark in the snow. A nice big crew, come from Montreal and offering premium job contracts to people in the community. Provided that they could deliver crew members to various locations spread across the territory surrounding the reserve. The pay was tempting and Nish had a snowmobile. Two, in fact: her father was also working on the production, as a scout.

"Nish, go do the run, we gotta keep our image hunters happy."

"Miam nutau..." Dad!

Her *nutau* was always accommodating, while she always felt like fighting, not with her fists but with her big mouth. But who's impressed by a nineteen-year-old kid? Not her father, that's for sure. Yet this was the one and only reason why she would head back to the film crew after having reached the convoy of vehicles. A gang of shivering Montrealers who forget their coffee in sub-zero temperatures. *But no, the cameraman certainly wouldn't be the one going to get the coffee, nor would he be the one going to get cigarettes for the big-shot producer from Montreal!*

"And none of those roll-your-owns or those Indian ciga-rettes, if you please."

Tedious goddamn joke. She'd restrained herself so that she wouldn't tell him he could take his fucking cigarettes and shove them.

"*Tshimai…*" Screw that…

By the time the crew realized they had forgotten the box with the cigarettes, they had already arrived at her uncle's hunting camp, where the day's work would be done.

"Nish will go," her father had said, leaving, as they say, little room for discussion.

But the job paid well and she had even made some friends among them.

The day was spectacular but the air was biting. When your cheeks are warmed by the sun but your lungs are scorched by the cold, life is good. Nish relaxed a bit. She might as well enjoy her outing at Montreal's expense.

It wouldn't be long before the truck would appear in the distance, as if it had been dropped right in the middle of the tundra, the only indication that a road ran behind the bank of snow. That and the Hydro poles. The sun was bouncing off the vehicles' windows from so far away that she could watch her snowmobile's reflection growing bigger over the last kilo-metre of tundra.

She was certainly not going back to the village to get Mr. Big Shot's cigarettes. *Nutau* had a pack stashed in the glove compartment. They were as dry as hay but they would do for now. *Nutau* hadn't smoked for at least nine years but he always kept a pack in the pickup truck in case he had to make an offering of tobacco. Nish remembered the day when he decided to quit. She was ten years old and had just been caught smoking with her cousin behind the church rectory. *Nutau* had delivered a lecture so long and tedious that the paint on the walls at home had surely chipped faster than it

9

usually did. The whole thing had ended in shared laughter when he concluded the lesson with a firm "No more smoking" as he himself was lighting a cigarette. That very day, she and her father had both decided to stop smoking. That was the thing she loved best about her *nutau*: he was consistent and always set a good example.

It was time to join the crew again. She would arrive just before the midday meal, which would give her plenty of time to steep the tea in the cast-iron kettle and unwrap the lunch that her mother and aunt had prepared the night before. Bannock, egg sandwiches, raw veggies…plenty of solid fare to fuel them for the rest of the afternoon without making them sleepy. That, in addition to serving them the litres of coffee she had just loaded into the sled attached to her snowmobile.

The return trip looked like it would be less pleasant than her trip there. The wind that had been at her back was colder, carving its path directly into her ears and making her cry icy tears. She wanted to lower her chin, but that would have left her driving blind, which is ill-advised, even in the vast expanse of the tundra. Nish saw snow clouds approaching from a long way away but it didn't really worry her. She was sure that the snow wouldn't reach them until nightfall and by then they would have packed everything up to get back on the road, so the day would not be lost. But she simply could not travel the rest of the way headfirst into the wind.

Nish decided to take a short detour that followed a sinuous little river and opened up into the lake. She veered off to the right. Not only would she lose the headwind that was making the route difficult, but the path she knew ran along a mountainside that offered shelter from the wind. And it was such a beautiful landscape. There was a little waterfall to cross, but in winter it provided safe passage for her snowmobile. She knew the place well since she had spent a number of days there, fishing with her family. Her father and uncle, who climbed up the trail with the canoe on their backs, told her each time how the ancestors had also gone up this trail in the fall, taking the entire family with them, the women carrying packs and provisions for the coming winter. Then they came back down the same way in the spring.

This was the history of all the Innu born on the Nitassinan. Her father and uncle had both made the ascent to their land when they were young. The tradition was broken when her father was obliged to follow the path his brother had taken to boarding school. In the summer, they lived in the village because that's where everyone from the community met in the warm season, at the traditional fishing grounds. The children returning from boarding school felt disconnected from the restless excitement of their parents, who were preparing for a new season in the forest. They were like two paths running in diametrically opposite directions. Her grandparents had made the annual trip up to the fishing grounds three more times before permanently settling in the village. Their sons were then able to go to the White school in the neighbouring village and come back home every night. Nish's father recalled this period, before the boarding school, as the happiest of his childhood. He always said that he had been lucky to go up to their land when he was old enough to remember it and before the priest intervened with his parents and forced him to leave. They had fudged a bit about his age but, like all the community's children, he'd finally had to resign himself to leaving his parents for several months. But what he had learned and experienced on that portion of their territory had stayed with him. His uncle's camp sat at the same place where his family had left for the territory for decades or – according to certain oral histories – for centuries.

Nish had always loved the light that elongated the shadows of the spruce trees when the sun was setting or when the thaw unleashed the waterfall and the water ran peacefully between the rocks. She began the ascent on her snowmobile, the machine's nose rising to the rhythm of the drifts that had been left there by the last snowstorm, as if it was devouring the powdery snow that hadn't yet hardened in the cold. The row of trees to her right meant she didn't have to worry about an accidental tumble into the frozen river below. At the very worst, she would have gently slid toward this straight line of trees, which would have kept her fall from proving fatal, but getting back up would have been a nightmare! The trail was suitable for a safe portage, though it would leave a man lugging a canoe and paddles on his back a little out of breath.

Nish considered herself lucky that it was her means of transportation that carried her up the hill and not the other way around. Once at the top, she was able to assess the valley and the second slope that rose before her. She used the momentum of her descent to get a good start up the next hill, but as she rounded the bend, she saw an obstacle that shouldn't have been there: a series of trees that had fallen across the route that she was planning to take. Lying on the ground like the spokes of a fan, they blocked at least three metres of the trail, with some of the treetops dangling over the void, thus barring her way.

She found herself facing a blowdown, trees uprooted by strong winds. She thought for a moment and wondered if she could ride over it, but decided that this was not an option. Going around it to the right would be too dangerous and the thought of having to go the left wasn't very encouraging either. She would have to zigzag through the trees and make a big detour to avoid the blowdown, but she would probably be able to get back on the trail a little further on and continue making her way to the camp.

Nish got off the snowmobile and set off on the trail toward the left, steering with both hands and trying to guide the heavy machine across the trees so that the skis would not get stuck between dead branches.

She was able to skirt a few trees, but the climb was exhausting. Her feet constantly sank into the snow and her arms were beginning to tire from guiding the snowmobile and its fully loaded sled across the loosely packed snow. After several metres of battling the uncooperative stuff, she was already deep into the forest that crowned the top of the little mountain and had lost sight of the thin light coming from falls behind her. Each metre gained stole a bit more of her breath, but she was determined to go around the obstacle to get back on the trail a little further away. She had already gone too far in this direction to turn back now.

When the beginning of a clearing appeared through the trees, she was sure that her troubles were over. The snow indicated that there was a geological fold under the blanket of white. She moved forward, certain that the path would soon be more accessible, and even climbed back onto her snowmobile. No sooner had she reached the summit of the powdery knoll than her heart sank at the sight of the gaping fissure that opened up before her. A gash in the rock itself left an exposed stone wall on her right and a steep slope under her feet. As she tried to fight the laws of gravity by digging her boots into the snow, the metal mass and its cargo naturally began to hurtle down the sharp incline. Nish tried to propel herself off the leather seat with a kick, but she was caught by the well-attached sled following behind. As she fell, she grazed an inclusion in the rock wall and heard a loud tearing sound from the lower part of her body. A broken leg? Torn pants? She didn't know yet but prayed that when she stopped falling, the second possibility would prove to be the case.

Two seconds before hitting the ground, she saw the snowmobile sink into the snow and disappear as if diving into a pool of feathers, thereby completely vanishing from sight. She hoped that her landing would be as soft but the signs did not bode well. She hit the snowmobile still hidden under the snow feet first, confirming that it wasn't the sound of cloth tearing she'd just heard. She had just enough time to feel the pain of her broken leg before her head hit the buried metal machine.

She inhaled a bit of snow, which melted in her throat. She was cold, but it wasn't the end of the world; fortunately for her, she had dressed in her snowsuit that morning. *My life for a bowl of hot soup... I don't think I can...*

...

My head is killing me...

...

Why are they pressing on my head?
"Hello? Is someone there..."

A gentle shaking, followed by another. Nish opened her eyes to find that the sun had given way to a dark blue sky, and snowflakes were wafting gently through the tops of the spruce. Another tremor moved the trees. She raised her head for a better view of what had created this pulsation. Then two little grey lights danced before her eyes before disappearing into the blackness.

A shower of dust and earth fell on her face. Nish tried to move, only to receive more dust on her head and down her neck. A wave of panic washed over her. Had she been buried alive? The enveloping cold cast back the humidity of her breath.

"Aaaaahhhhhhhhhh! Help!"

The sound reverberated against the earthen wall. She squirmed around so that she could see how tightly she was wedged. Her entire upper body was squeezed into a space with a scarce 10 centimetres of wiggle room. She noted that she could move her left leg rather freely, but the right throbbed painfully and seemed strangely rigid. She raised her good foot, trying to assess the amount of free space she had. Nish used all the strength of her uninjured foot and slid out of the minuscule space in which she'd been stuck. Feeling her way, she explored the area and the cold, damp earth, which to her surprise was not completely frozen. She guessed that the available space was about the size of a car. She was able to sit up in the surrounding darkness. She felt hampered by the damaged leg: when she touched it, her calf felt like it was wrapped in a roll of cardboard.

A few minutes passed and she waited for her eyes to adjust to the absence of light. Nothing changed. She was in total darkness. She rooted through her pocket for her cell phone but didn't feel it. Then she remembered the inside pocket and the pack of cigarettes she'd been sent to get. Maybe she'd get lucky and... Bingo! Slipped into the packet: matches! She took her time so as not to waste them.

Then there was light and Nish could finally study her surroundings. As borne out by her first impressions, she saw that the space was limited: an angled surface made of decomposing but still-whole logs formed a low wall that differed greatly from the other walls, which seemed to be composed of humus. A round granite boulder stood out in a corner. Light from the second match revealed her cell phone on the ground where she had awakened. She could keep the precious matches for later and use the cell phone's glow instead. By some inexplicable miracle, the screen was intact even though the glass had once cracked when her phone had simply fallen out of her pocket. She thanked her lucky stars.

She looked down at her leg and saw that a roll of birchbark was protecting it. She'd heard talk of birchbark splints, but she'd never seen one and had certainly never made one. She must have hit her head very hard if she didn't remember having made this splint. She couldn't walk on her leg but she would carefully protect it until she could get it treated at the hospital. She must have been really motivated to rip the bark off a birch without a hatchet...but in any case, she'd found the perfect protection to keep from bumping or bending her ankle any more than necessary.

She continued her perusal of the space. This wasn't a bear's cave since the odour of decomposing vegetation would never lead her to believe that an animal had used it as its lair. So she left to the realm of the imagination the crazy possibility that a bear had awakened from its hibernation to store her there as an end-of-season snack. She searched for the way out because, to have ended up here, she must have slid, semiconscious, through some kind of hole. She saw that just next to the rock, the decomposing matter was less uniform and that the snow had cascaded down in the same spot. She tested the strength of the wall and the snow gave way beneath her hand. Using both hands, she dug out the snow and rotting branches that seemed to have clogged the entrance tunnel. Trying not to put weight on her leg, she slid into the hole leading upward to a way out of her dark shelter. The cold wind filled her lungs with a welcome freshness.

Outside, night had fallen. Nothing of her surroundings could be seen in the midnight blackness. She used her cell phone's flashlight app to look around. The light reflected clearly off the thickly falling snowflakes that she'd felt on her face even before she'd seen them. But visibility was no more than two metres. She raised her phone to the sky and realized that she had no network access: how typical! If there was one thing she knew only too well, it was that you do not leave a safe place if you might end up sorry you can't find it again once you're 10 metres away. She could make out the place where she had crawled to the shelter's entrance but the traces would be no more than a memory by morning. She had to remember the direction to take from the entrance because her snowmobile lay waiting at the end of that path. A second check of her cell phone confirmed that the mountain's rocky flanks were separating her from the joys of the Internet. Well, okay, at least she knew she was alive. First bit of good news. Second bit of good news, she had fire. First bit of bad news, she was hungry – but it wasn't serious, just unpleasant. Having snow meant she had water and, until morning, it would suffice.

For the moment, it was important to keep fear from getting the upper hand. The news was always reporting on people who disappeared in the forest and the dramatic consequences. Fear in the forest either paralyzes you or makes you do dangerous things. With her upper body still rising out of the hole in the snow, Nish took another look around and tried to locate some kindling to burn for warmth in her little hideout. She lay on her belly and slid toward a young fir tree and broke off all the branches big enough for her purposes. A fallen spruce tree lay at her side, its top peaking out like a head capped by a layer of accumulated snow. She grabbed the top of the dead tree and shook it as she pulled. Nish had no trouble sliding it toward the entrance of her cave. She pushed the fir branches in first. She looked for a foothold in the snow, climbed on top of the tree's skeleton and broke it with her knee. The parts too big to be broken were stripped of their tiny branches and Nish was able to bring the bouquet of sticks and broken branches into the shelter, leaving the bigger pieces of wood outside near the entrance.

She eased herself back inside, feet first, so that she could loosely cover the hole behind her. She would have to go out again but, more importantly, she would have to let some air in so that she wouldn't suffocate as she slept. She put her phone on the ground, face up with the screen lit. She would use the flashlight app only if necessary. Since the battery was only 75 per cent charged, she would have to use it sparingly until she could make a call the next day, when conditions would be better.

She carefully shook the branches, removing the snow from those that would serve as firewood for the night. Already the scent and comfort they provided calmed her, and she told herself that tonight would just be like a night spent camping on her people's land. A little iron pan would have certainly been welcome, but she would try using stones heated in the fire instead. She had never seen it done but had heard talk of it. It was akin to the way the grandfathers prepared big stones for the sweat, only without an immense outdoor fire. Her fire would be inside the shelter, and she considered using the boulder in the corner. She had no idea if this would work, but it was better than nothing.

She balanced her small collection of branches on the exposed part of the rock and lit those that, despite the snow still clinging to their bark, crackled as the resin heated up. Nish even peeled several layers of bark off her splint to help get the fire started. As the fire grew stronger, Nish used a branch to make sure that the pile of embers stayed safely perched on the rock. If only she could get rid of her pounding headache! She'd been able to ignore it, but now that the adrenalin-charged panic was dissipating, she increasingly felt her heartbeats as they tried to escape through her temples. She searched the coat pocket that held her slim wallet and wondered if she still had some ibuprofen. Within the folds, tucked deep in a crease in the leather, hid a packet that had already been opened. She unfolded the dirty paper to find half a tablet. Better than nothing. She swallowed it with a bit of saliva. The little fire burned quickly and gave off a certain warmth, but nothing would turn her hole in the ground into a luxury hotel. She hoped that the heat would accumulate in the rock and then spread. She tossed the scrap of paper and a few old receipts into the fire and they were immediately consumed. When she touched the rock, she fully understood that her plan had failed. The rock was hot where the fire was burning but, like an iceberg, the major portion of the rock lay beneath the frozen ground. It probably would have worked with a smaller rock. Adding pieces of wood, she let the flames heat the air.

Nish lay down on her pine twigs and gazed at the discreet flame that lit her makeshift dwelling. She was, in any case, lucky to have this hideaway. She'd have to have X-rays when she got back to town, where they would take care of her leg and check to see if her head was all right, that she hadn't cracked her skull. She must have suffered serious trauma if she couldn't remember how she'd gotten there and who had applied her splint.

Her cold pine bed worked wonders on the pain beating in her temples. Suddenly, she was gripped by fear. What if she didn't make it through the night? What if she fell asleep in the frigid air, never to wake up? If she had an aneurysm and slipped into a coma? No one would ever find her. A shiver ran through her and she felt tears welling up. She knew she had to remain calm, but she allowed herself a brief moment of panic. She closed her eyes and began to pray. Her grandmother told her to always remember the spirits and Tshishe Manitu. Her *nukum* was very pious and never missed Mass. Nish was much less of a believer than her grandmother but she sometimes enjoyed going with her, just to hear her singing in Innu at church. So she focused on her grandmother as she prayed, letting the old woman's image soothe her and direct her toward happier thoughts.

Nish opened her eyes to the same total darkness she'd been in with her eyes closed. She was cold, very cold. A tremendous shiver shook her body. She put her hand into her pocket to find the precious matchbook. She had to relight the little rock fire, which had since died out. Feeling for it with her fingers, she pulled at the paperboard in the pack of cigarettes to use as kindling. After emptying the pack's contents on the ground, she began tearing up the flimsy board. She lit the first match. It took two seconds for her eyes to adjust to the light and just one more to realize that the two black beads staring at her were eyes in the middle of a face. She screamed so loudly that her vocal cords had no time to synchronize with the air leaving her lungs. Her fingers dropped the little flame illuminating the face. With all the strength her limbs allowed, she tried to back away from creature that had been watching her. She heard gentle rustlings moving about the shelter. She screamed again as fear made her forget where the way out was. She felt something brush against her leg. She jumped in the opposite direction, frantically searching for her cell phone and the light that would help her find the exit. The screen's backlighting showed her the creature, which was still staring at her intensely from its position right in front of the shelter's exit. She would have thrown up if her stomach hadn't been empty. She cried uncontrollably, unable to think clearly in the presence of this being, which was taking its sweet time looking at her. It wasn't an animal nor was it a monster, at least not in the traditional meaning of the word. The thing resembled a seven- or eight-year-old child in size and appearance. But it was not a child, it wasn't even human. Its eyes were big for its head and were totally black, like the eyes you see in horror movies. The most bizarre part, the thing that proved to her that she was not in the company of a child, was the colour and texture of its skin, which reminded her of a grey trout, although the speckles were much less conspicuous.

Nish was in the presence of something she simply could not explain, her brain seemingly unwilling to process the information. The creature, hunkered down by the shelter's egress, remained stoic and did not take its eyes off Nish. Nish dared not make the first move since she had no way of knowing the risk she would be taking, and with one leg out of commission, the odds were not in her favour.

The staredown must have lasted for 15 minutes, the creature motionless and Nish trying to understand. She was well versed in the Atshens' legends but this thing did not appear to be a giant man-eating monster. In all the stories about tiny people that appeared and played tricks on hunters, they were described as mini-humans but there was nothing to the effect that their skin was like a trout's. The thing seemed to be calmer than Nish; it had some kind of fur on its back, but nothing Nish could identify. From its crouching position, the creature kept its eyes glued to Nish. Then it turned its head toward the fire before taking one last look at the young woman. The creature raised its arm and gestured toward the mound of kindling wood. Seeing no reaction from Nish, it began signaling in the fire's direction again. Sensing no hostility, Nish slid over toward the extinguished fire. Using its little spotted hands, the creature made the young woman understand that she must create a flame.

Nish reassembled the twigs and scraps of paper from the pack of cigarettes. She took another match and struck it against the cover. The flame grew as soon as the match touched wood. Nish gave a little cry when the creature came near. It grabbed Nish's wrist and snatched the matchbook from her hand. The creature's strength was the greatest surprise. It was incredibly strong! Nish could never have kept her matches, even if she'd wanted to. In any case, she wouldn't risk attacking the creature, who had just proven that she had done well not to underestimate the precariousness of her situation.

Nish kept the fire going as the thing studied the packet it'd just taken from her. Then it slipped it away, making the packet disappear under its fur. The fire bathed the shelter in warm light. The relative peace that had settled in was interrupted by a rustling coming from the tunnel leading out. Was another one of these burrowing things coming into the cave? The snow blocking the entryway gave way beneath the little black paws entering the cave. These paws were attached to a fox. The magnificent animal entered and did a brief tour of the space, even smelling Nish as it went by. It then went to lie down behind the creature, yawning before resting its head on its forelegs. The creature rose, went to the mouth of the tunnel, filled the hole back up with snow and then returned to its place beside the fox.

Nish thought that the situation could not be any odder. The fox raised its head, approached Nish and sniffed at the wall to her right. The animal began scratching at the earth and digging with two paws, continually smelling the frozen dirt. The fox's activity uncovered what appeared to be a piece of fabric. Nish watched and wondered what was making the little beast so excited. The fox dug and dug at the hole and, all of a sudden, it dislodged a dirt-covered parcel. The fox looked in vain for a way to open it. The creature stood, walked up to the bundle, took it in its hands and opened it. The exterior was made of several thicknesses of birchbark; its center held something reddish-brown that looked like pieces of wood stacked in the hollow left by the sheets of bark. The creature reached into the pile and gave the first piece to the fox, who took it between its jaws and began gnawing it with sharp teeth. The creature took a piece into its little grey-lipped mouth and held another out to Nish, who looked at it, smelled it and then slipped it into her mouth. Dried meat! How was that possible? She looked at the hole and then at the meat. It had almost no taste and she hadn't detected any odour, but she recognized the distinct texture of dried caribou. She approached the hole the fox had dug and grabbed the fabric that had been unearthed, noticing how much it reminded her of the old cotton canvas that prospectors used to make their tents. She pulled, but the fabric was firmly stuck in the wall. She pulled again with all the strength her arms had to give, but to no avail. The creature came over and took a turn. A few more shakes and, thanks to the little being's hidden strength, the fabric slowly appeared. When the creature could not work any more of the fabric free, it went back over to her fox – *her* fox, because, given the trust they each showed for the other, it was definitely the creature's animal.

The stitching that could be seen on the side confirmed Nish's impression that this was an old tent. She turned back toward her fire and fed it a bit more; she could not let it die now that she had used her last match. The fox grabbed another piece of meat and went back to curl up next to the creature, who was still chewing on its own piece. Nish preferred not to eat this old meat since her hunger was not so great that she would risk eating spoiled food. She stretched out, the fatigue from all her emotions beginning to weigh on her. How could she explain all this? She even began to wonder if she hadn't died and gone to the other side.

The two beings before her rose as soon as they'd finished their meal and crept toward Nish. She was dumbfounded when the fox lay down at her feet and the creature lay down against her like a child resting in the crook of its parent's arms. But Nish's biggest surprise was the discovery that the little thing was pregnant. The belly that bulged from its furry underside left no doubt about it. Nish lay still and felt the heat emanating from the mother-to-be. Although she had heard the legends about the mystery that came from their land, she simply never thought that she would one day see it for herself. She laid her head on the arm that she had extended beneath her. The magic of legends, or the natural world that we too easily forget... Legends...

When she opened her eyes again, Nish saw the shelter in a new way, thanks to white light now filtering in through the opening in the snow. But where was the creature? The fox? She looked around and saw only emptiness. She assumed that they had left through the cleared tunnel and so she did the same. Outside, the blinding sun was reflected off the new snow. She searched the surroundings for her companions, but she saw only the relatively fresh tracks of a fox winding between the spruce trees. She tried to spot the creature, but in vain. She scanned the area and could make out her shelter, its flat side and the curved portion. She noticed that the snow had been disturbed. She slid toward what must be the roof of her hideout. The digging had freed the other side of the canvas, which had been extricated by the fox and the creature, and it now lay beneath her. She took a closer look and pulled on a huge piece of birch bark, which came loose from the wooden ribs...of a canoe! A lightbulb went off in Nish's head. She was on top of a cache that had collapsed. Underneath her lay an expedition's leftover supplies that had never been retrieved! A piece of bark had been torn from the side of the canoe. Her splint! But how? How? She was racked with enormous doubt: had the creature dragged her there to take care of her? It was too incredible for her to believe. She began to cry because she knew that no one else would believe her either.

A throbbing hum in the distance softly filled the sky. Could it be snowmobiles? As the sound from above made her aware that it was probably a helicopter, she realized that she was in the worst possible place to be spotted from the air. She pulled on the skin of the canoe, which she straddled. Using her good leg, she began to slide along the snow toward the clearing below...

HANNIBALO-GOD-MOZILLA AGAINST THE GREAT COSMIC VOID

Louis-Karl Picard-Sioui
Wendat from Wendake

The force of impact is calculated according to the velocity of the vehicle when it collides with the noble beast's immovable body. Troubling: despite what the sign says, it cannot quantify the distance in these two kilometres. The moose is just massive enough to cause creative chaos. The boiling-hot asphalt buckles the road. A strident silence announces the beginning of the performance. A secret song, a hymn to violence. The crimson chrome explodes. The shards of glass scatter across the blazing bitumen. They illustrate the most exquisite facets of the pain. The vehicle's body bellows one last time under an insolent sun. Your own body was hemmed in tight. Now, it's everywhere. Here and there.

This is your most beautiful painting and you'll never know it.

April 19, 1985

Soon it will be my birthday. Again. No point in rushing, good things come to those who wait. For a fist that blackens your left eye. Or rather, your right: it's on the left when you look in the mirror. I get them confused sometimes. I wonder whether the real world is not actually the one in the glass. Some say that the mirror gives access to another world, the world of spirits. Kitchike's Elders say the opposite. That mirrors keep the wraiths at bay. They're afraid of their reflection. I look at myself and tell myself that maybe I'm a spirit too. Because I don't like to see myself in the mirror. Especially when my face is badly bruised. Mother says that it's the same thing every year: I get peevish a few days before my birthday. I grouse and get into squabbles at school. I do everything I'm not supposed to do. Mother says lots of things that I'm sure I'll learn to respect one day. For the moment, I couldn't care less. I certainly feel guilty during the 32-hour sermon she inflicts on me each time, but, contrary to her expectations, the lecture does not seem to stick. No way am I going to let someone call me *kawish*, even if, just like that little snot Sylvain who spat the word in my face, I have no idea what it means. But the tone with which he flung his venom clearly indicated that it was an insult.

"*Kawishhhhh!*"

I wonder if it's spelled with an *e*?

October 12, 2007

I met this girl, Éliane. A girl from the North. Still and always the North. Tonight, we talk about movies. She tells me about the love affair she had with Elliott when she was young. Elliott and his mountain of stuffed animals. I remember *E.T.* very well. Mother took me to the city to see this Spielberg masterpiece when I was a kid. I'd been stunned by cinema's inherent truth, and my relationship to time was changed forever. Not because of the film as such. I remember getting there late. The first in a long series of late arrivals. We had missed the beginning of the showing, but that was a minor issue because after the final credits, the movie started again as if it had no beginning or end. My mind navigated between the cosmic cycle of eternity and an uninterrupted line of Smarties that served as bait for an exosystemic Pac-Man. It was my first postmodern experience. I was eight years old.

August 28, 1990

There's a rerun of *The Dog Who Stopped the War* on TV. "War, war, that's no reason to get hurt!" During the advertisements, they show news flashes. Balaclava-wearing Aboriginals equipped with Chinese imitations of Russian-made automatic weapons are spreading terror south of Montreal. The people want bread and circuses, but the wicked Indians refuse to share their cemetery so that the golf course can be expanded. Once again, the city is beleaguered by the bloodthirsty savages of history books. The great return of the Iroquois, those ghosts from another time who refuse to disappear before French-Montreal's Holy Empire. Kahnawake, a village of diehards surrounded by the Gallic colony of Bourrassites. The poor colonists on the South Shore watch the same channel as I do. When the movie is over, they go out into the street and throw dirt at the Elders and the children fleeing the reserve. Except that it's summer, so they throw rocks instead.

"*Kawiiiiishhhh!*"

March 23, 1998

My heart is in tatters, I have no appetite. I'm nauseated by the mere thought of swallowing any food whatsoever. I am gutted. A gaping black hole has taken refuge inside me. Three years, less three months, less three days. That's how long my youthful love lasted. Stéphanie. Her name is

Stéphanie Yaskawich. She woke up this morning and she no longer loved me. It's Thursday. Garbage night. She decided to clean the house, then to clean out the house. It was her turn to take the garbage cans to the curb and, while she was at it, she kicked me to the curb along with them. With no anger, no hate. The most natural thing in the world. She said, "Thank you, Charles, for these wonderful years. But the two of us are finished. Over and done. I don't love you anymore." And so I left. I pummelled the garbage cans with my fists, just to mock myself for being there, just for having existed. Mother says that I'm worth more than that. That I have a brilliant future ahead of me. That Stéphanie's the one losing out. I realize that I'd been wrong, finally. I've grown up a lot, but I still couldn't care less what Mother says. But still I'm happy that she says it.

July 13, 1983
Summer brings its share of fun for Kitchike's kids. A crowd overruns the main street, little kiosks line up in a row, and feathers are brightly coloured. It's the powwow. Bright-eyed tourists, children with their balloons, Father Pinault's cassock and his embroidered moosehide stole, the Indian princess and her brave on horseback... And the mascots: Yogi Bear's brother, the chief in his feathered outfit, the local troupe that competes with the neighbouring city's gang of rejects and their Fur Festival. And as a bonus, this summer we have E.T. The one-and-only, the real E.T. Yippee! E.T. came back, I knew he would. He stretched out his index finger with its firefly tip and called the band council to announce his big comeback. Then, like all the aristocratic and royal assholes since Lord Durham, he decided to make his first public appearance at the Kitchike powwow.

God Bless the Queen!
God Bless the Alien!
God Bless the fucking powwow!

September 1, 2012

I'm sitting on my left buttock, my back crooked, my hip against the back of the chair, my legs splayed out to the side, and I wonder why. Why I cannot beat the odds. Why I am still staring at my screen instead of sitting up straight. Or better still, standing up, putting on my jacket and going out, escaping this prison that our apartment is too quickly becoming when I'm caught between one status and another, that of agoraphilic co-dependent and that of single father. Everything is on the kitchen table. I have nowhere else to set up. I stare at the screen and see my reflection. I've aged, but it's still me. The same look in the eyes, the same crooked nose that pulls to the left. I mean to the right: it pulls to the right in the mirror. I still get it mixed up. But I always feel the insult when I touch it. A souvenir from a teenagers' fist fight. Probably on the eve of my birthday. It's hard to remember. I increase the screen's brightness and my reflection fades. The light dispels the darkness and restores the balance of power.

Wait, once again the question intrudes on my thoughts. I have a tangle of memories, the kind we all have when we contemplate our first years of life. What was really and truly the first movie I saw in the theatre? *The Muppets Take Manhattan*, *E.T.* or *The Empire Strikes Back*? I could have spent the rest of my life asking the question, trying to convince myself that it's merely a detail, a footnote in the history of my existence. But tonight, I decided to stop being the victim of the hazy nature of my early memories. So I take matters in hand and google the years of theatrical releases.

The Empire Strikes Back: 1980.
E.T.: 1982.
The Muppets Take Manhattan: 1984.

This may explain my fascination with *Star Wars*. Ask my son about it. Just as I come to this realization, a whole new question arises: what if it wasn't *E.T.* that I'd seen out of order, opening scene after the final credits? The more I think about it, the more I think it was the Muppets. And I don't know if it's because I was little back then, but I envision a giant Hannibal destroying the city like Godzilla, his little left-butt-cheek cousin (probably sitting all crooked on the chair, like me). And I realize I'm thinking that Godzilla is the godlike and monstrous version of Mozilla, the non-profit company that programs the Web browser I use to google movie-release dates. And I think that maybe it's Hannibalo-God-Mozilla's fault that I waste so much time obsessing in front of my computer and wandering around the Interweb instead of going out and contributing to society. Surely it was written in my tender youth, this life of constantly browsing – with no beginning or end – the countless possibilities.

And should I dare to disconnect, would I finally be set free?

February 6, 2011
Big black eyes stare at me, mesmerized, as my gaping mouth dispatches an endless stream of spiteful words. I am Hannibal, smashing the Manhattan skyscraper in an outpouring of rage. My fists descend on the walls, the table and everything that would hurt me. But I feel nothing. Nothing but the pain of being in the world, lost at the outer limits of rage, prisoner of my internal emptiness. My little treasure howls his inability to understand. I hardly hear the words escaping from

Éliane's mouth: "This's why I didn't talk to you about it before. You scare me when you're like this." She slams the door and disappears under Tatooine's setting suns.

She has met someone. Someone else. A sundancer from the North. Tonight, she'll talk about movies with him, make plans. They'll do the powwow circuit, visit Navajo country. They'll watch her chick flicks under the covers. They'll make love while I watch her sister empty out our place. Suddenly, I feel the full force of Alderaan's destruction and I collapse on the sofa. I extend my arms toward the little clone that she bore, embrace him tenderly. I don't know if it's for reassurance or for comfort. But I avoid looking him in the eye. I avoid fuelling the abyss.

December 8, 1981
I'm lying in my bed, curled up and trembling under a mountain of blankets. I share the room with Colin, my imaginary friend, and an assembly of stuffed animals strewn here and there on the floor. The toy Elders are displayed on shelves along the wall. Unlike their lower-status cousins, they are all topsy-turvy and grey with dust. Some have belonged to several generations of my family. Members of the stuffed-toy council have the honour of standing guard while I sleep. Colin told me so because the Elders do not speak to me.

I asked Colin to intercede on my behalf. For a week now, a new addition to the furry folk has kept me awake. The Mad Hatter. A bit of printed felt attached to a wooden stick. A souvenir from the Ice Capades. His big eyes observe my slightest movements, day and night. The minute I close my eyes, he wreaks havoc in my room. He plays innocent, remaining motionless with his mocking smile, but I know. I am totally convinced that he is concocting a diabolical plan to overthrow the Elders. What's worse: he knows that I know.

Obviously, I didn't tell Mother about it. She would never believe me. "Oh, Charles, come on! You have an overactive imagination!" she'd say. I didn't discuss it with Mother, but I did with Colin. Even he thought I was exaggerating. "It's just a scrap of felt, Charlie. He can't do anything against the power of the Elders."

Just the same, the previous night, when I was going to sleep, I heard him breathing. I swear to you on my Atari, I heard his voice just as I was entering dreamland. He whispered, like a breeze:

"Kawish! *Kaaaawishhhhh!*"

January 1, 2009

It's 2 in the morning and I'm in the city, in a half-deserted hospital, tears in my eyes, heart as wide as the sky and my spirit light. In my arms, tenderly swaddled in his little green blanket, is my son. A pure being, so beautiful in all his fragility. A being made in the image of the North, the image of his mother. My contentment is so profound, so complete that I weep it out with all the water from my body. Mother never told me that feeling such happiness can make you cry. My progeny in my arms, I float through the grey corridors toward a nursing station where he is entitled to get his first needle prick. Standard tests, apparently. The first in a long line, if I can rely on my own medical records. I follow the blue dots on the floor. The light blue ones. You must pay attention because the dark ones lead somewhere else. I follow the Smarties, one by one, and dream of the moment when I can finally call the house and tell Mother everything. If only I too had an index finger with a firefly tip.

April 20, 1978
I sit, alone at the table. In front of me, a Jos Louis cake
bearing two candles. The house is upside down. A few rays
of sun penetrate the broken window, making the dust motes
dance in the air. The chairs are overturned, the floor covered with debris, broken bottles and perfectly round
droplets of blood that draw a path from one room to the
next.

Mother says that you must always save the reds for last.
But for now, she says nothing. Nothing intelligible, at least.
She cries, wails, moans. She beseeches all the spirits and all
the saints. A faceless man pursues her through the house. He
throws at her everything that he finds along the way, which is
mainly empty bottles of O'Keefe. After a minute, he catches
her and pins her against the counter. As he delivers a hail of
blows, he bellows like a madman. He strikes and strikes again
until Mother collapses on the floor.

I should be screaming too. I should be horrified by so
much violence. But the truth is that I feel nothing. Absolutely
nothing. I just wonder what Mother had done to deserve such
punishment. To go from his "beautiful Indian princess" to a
"fucking *kawish* who doesn't care about anything but her li'l
bastard."

The faceless man slams the door. Of the house. On his
family. On my life. I take the candles out of the cake and
offer Colin a piece. He's not hungry. Neither am I. But I'm
a good boy. So I eat anyway, in case the man comes back
with balloons.

Almost now
I often catch myself getting lost in the metatext of my own
existence, where I can be subject, object and result of my

autoethnobiographical research all at once. However, I have never put it down in writing and will never have another chance to do so. I thought Mother deserved at least that much. To know how much I love her. That it isn't her fault. That she always did her best, what she believed was right, even when it was too much. She was always so proud of me. I hope that she'll accept the results of my analysis. My last opus. The most sacred and most brilliant of my creations: my final production. I must not fail because there'll be no second chance. A single performance to demonstrate all my glory. To shine one last time, one first time, before I die.

People tell me: "You, Charles, are a genius." They're actually serious. I say it's a load of crap. Crap that massages the ego when you occasionally need to lie to yourself, but crap all the same. I learned some time ago that my way of thinking, my cerebral operating system, is unlike other people's.

Some time ago
I realize that my cerebral operating system is unlike that of others. Although we often have the same cultural references and share, theoretically, the same universe, my mind does not process data in the same fashion and thus does not arrive at the same conclusions, nor does it present them in the same way. I believe that this is due to the reconfiguration of the brain's arborescence, which I had to manage at a very young age to circumvent a central element of my personality's binary code, thus forcing me to convert my system to quantum mode and to calculate all possibilities on the basis of an exclusively feminine matrix. Some think that this has turned me into an intelligent person. I must confess that, while it gives me a certain originality, it creates all sorts of pathetic anxieties that render me powerless when faced with a host of

little everyday things that many consider to be the abecedarium of resourcefulness.

Whoa.

The sofa isn't sturdy enough to support the weight of my musings, so I crawl to my bed, soaked to the bone. In my head, I hear Grandmother. I thank her for being there every day, even since her great departure. I spare a thought for my Mother, my son, his mother. And all the women who acted as a mother to me, even if they weren't. And I realize what luck I've had, having so many mothers. And I bless the women of Kitchike and of all our Nations. I hold sacred all the women in the universe.

But at the same time, I realize that this isn't enough. It was never enough. No matter how many mothers, the gaping hole in my deepest self has only grown as the years pass. No success, no victory, no adrenaline rush, no moment of absence lost in the Web, no character from the fictional worlds produced by Hollywood – not E.T. or Hannibal or the damn Ewoks – nothing, absolutely nothing could fill the void.

Now

I struggle to control myself. To stay awake. I'm nodding off, my mind has already begun navigating other realities. In rapid succession, each of the fractures in my existence shatters my consciousness. I let the last vial fall. I have swallowed enough pills to cure all the illnesses on the entire Earth and probably those on several planets in galaxies far, far away. I get dressed and grab my bag. No way am I going to croak between four walls. I set out on the path through the woods. Soon, Colin, I'll join you. Under the watchful eyes of the stuffed Elders, my soul will float down the grey corridors, then across the valleys, and I will follow the Smarties to La La Land, where there are no beginnings and no ends.

I took a few notes on things to do when I get to the other side. Top of the list: Sylvain, the little bully who hassled me in the schoolyard. I can still hear him, sometimes, when I close my eyes: *"Kawishhhh! Kaaaawishhhh!"* He was in a terrible accident last month. He was going through the park to get to the opening of his show when the sun blinked. His car took a moose to the windshield. It was all over the news. I promised myself I'd fuck him up as soon as I got there. If ever he comes back to life or is reincarnated, you can be sure that he'll never torment anyone again, the little shit.

I also had a vague thought about my grandfathers, whom I never got the chance to know. My mother always said that I resemble her father. I can't wait to see if, for once, I agree with her. One way or another, I imagine we'll have a lot of things to tell each other. And the last thing that comes to mind, as I cross the threshold of the door, the last thought before I lose consciousness, this final voluntary thought goes to my son. And I realize that, like me, he'll have to live with the vast abyss that eats you up inside. And I hope with all my heart that he will have enough mothers around him to fill the emptiness that I bequeath to him.

Sorry, son.

Papa has accounts to settle.

Somewhere else.

THE LAKOTA SHAMAN

VIRGINIA PÉSÉMAPÉO BORDELEAU
Cree-Métis from Rapide-des-Cèdres

Charlie came from a long line of shamans. His great-grand-
father, Strong Bear, was Sitting Bull's companion throughout all the setbacks that his people endured as they con-
tended with the colonists' strength and numbers, especially
with the Yankee soldiers who overran the country from east
to west like an endless swarm of locusts. His father was a
member of the first group of children to be scooped up and
confined to a boarding school. When the youngsters
returned to the reserve during vacations, an old sage helped
them reclaim their ancestors' rituals, far from the prying
eyes of the Missionary Priests who proliferated among the
Native Americans. It was thanks to this man that Charlie
was able to become a medicine man: his father had shared
the secret lessons he had learned over the course of those
summers.

Charlie's wife had left 10 days ago, taking with her their
sons and the wobbly furniture offered by friends and relatives
in the community. Feeling boxed in at Pine Ridge, an Oglala
Lakota reserve in South Dakota, Paula dreamt at night of her
family's territory in the immense spaces surrounding northern
Alberta's Great Slave Lake. She had loaded their pickup
truck, started the motor and driven off without a backward
glance. Charlie wondered if the truck had held up and if he
would find the courage to take to the road when it came time

for him to visit the children and try to convince his beloved to come back to him.

He pondered the beauty of the Cree woman, whom he had met five years earlier at one of those gatherings whose purpose is to revive elements of their original spirituality, which had been lost when they came into contact with White men and their boarding schools. When Paula smiled, you noticed only the luscious red lips that opened to reveal her perfect teeth; it was a smile that brightened the Sioux's heart. Now, no light glowed within his chest and even the stars failed to penetrate the darkness of his soul.

Charlie was bored. A well-known shaman, he was participating in the fifth spiritual conference in Tucson, Arizona, and for two hours he had been leading a group of participants who had been randomly assigned a clan when they arrived from all over Canada and the United States. Upon entering the hotel room where the seminar was being held, each person had drawn an animal totem written on a scrap of paper from the box placed by the door. Charlie served as the Chipmunks' guide.

Lost in thought, the Oglala crossed his legs and dangled his foot in the air. He was breaking a cardinal rule: stay connected to Mother Earth by keeping your feet firmly planted on the ground. A few people cleared their throats, ill at ease and hoping to attract his attention. But Charlie just crossed his arms, more distant than ever. The people had no idea that he had just graduated from university as a psychologist and that he had acquired this attitude during his years of training when he was trying to appear polite in front of his professors.

A Cheyenne had been droning on for 45 minutes about the need to preserve the pure blood of their people. *What a bunch of baloney*, thought the shaman. *Hasn't this guy ever heard of Hitler? I can't even tell him to shut his mouth, that's not*

*the way we do things and I have to let him have his say. Pure
blood? There'd be nobody left to attend our workshops...*

He sighed and looked at the audience, gauging the number of participants waiting to speak, then surreptitiously con-
sulted his watch. Another half-hour and the session would be
over. The man finally came to the end of his speechifying. His
neighbour thanked him and very diplomatically corrected
those of his comments that he found to be overstated. Charlie
chucked to himself. Knowing that he suffered from the "wear-
ing-two-hats" or the "caught-in-the-middle" syndrome, he was
enjoying himself until he heard the emotionally charged voice
of the last participant.

"My name is Julia. Charlie, how old are you?"

Baffled, he noticed that she was crying. Without thinking, he replied that he was 33. She was clearly of mixed
blood, pretty, and curvy in all the right places. Her gypsy
dress left one golden shoulder bare. The Sioux suddenly felt
a renewed interest in his work, put his foot down on the floor
and picked up his eagle feather, symbol of the Great Spirit,
which he had casually dropped beside his chair. He sat up
straight and gave her a look indicating that she should continue.

"Since the beginning of the workshop, I've felt a kinship
with you, and I sense a deep sadness. I wonder if I'm feeling
a sorrow supressed since my childhood, the death of my little
brother Harry, who'd be exactly your age today... I was so
young at the time, but I wonder if it's possible to relive such
an early loss."

Charlie's inner therapist came to the aid of the medicine
man. He was pleased with his knowledge of Freudian and
Jungian theories, and his deep warm voice – his most useful
asset, the one that never failed to charm the most recalcitrant
girls – filled the room. You see, Charlie was not handsome
from the physical point of view. His face looked as if it had

been quickly carved with a knife without refining the details, thus giving his head the look of a real Apache, like the ones seen in archival photographs. He was also cursed with a massive body.

"Of course, my sister, our traumas can be reawakened by a catalyzing event that makes us remember them. We are in a healing circle here, and I believe you have the sensitivity to pick up on the vibrations around you," he submitted.

Julia smiled at him and he realized she could almost be his wife's twin. Now troubled himself, his voice stuck in his throat. Since he could no longer smooth-talk her, he looked at his watch again and called an end to the meeting. People hurried toward him, wanting to hug him, but he excused himself for a moment and walked over to the young Métis woman. Even with her high heels, she barely stood as tall as his shoulder. He leaned toward her and asked, "Will you be going to the general assembly in the ballroom soon? I'd like to go on with our discussion."

How could she refuse to meet with a shaman interested in her suffering? Julia effusively accepted the invitation, blushing all the way up to her wavy hair, and told him she was with her brother and a girlfriend. The Lakota's face lit up: so there was no boyfriend waiting in the wings. Desire rose in him like water in a well after a dry spell – slowly but surely.

By the time she arrived at the ballroom with her friend Hélène in tow, the party was in full swing. She had changed into a new white dress that clung to her body, and Charlie's eyes lit up at the sight of her tanned skin, which reminded him of the oranges hanging from the trees in the hotel courtyard. Her radiant skin looked good enough to eat. He was swaying to the country music beat in the middle of a row of line dancers, spinning around and moving gracefully, his long braid flowing down his back. A Hopi colleague sporting the colourful costume of his people approached various women, spreading alarm through Charlie's heart. *That bastard, he's not going to steal her away from me!* he thought.

He raised his arm to greet Julia from across the room and made his way through the crowd. Trying to look as unruffled as possible, he walked toward the trio. Julia cheerfully introduced him to Hélène, a plump little brunette who was also from the French-speaking part of Canada, a province she specified as Quebec. The Sioux was relieved to see that the other shaman's amorous attentions were directed at Julia's friend.

"I came to tell you that I promised to eat with Hélène and my brother, and he's waiting for us at the restaurant where he made a reservation earlier today... We're on vacation, you know, so I asked Louis to take us on a walk early this morning to find the best places to eat after the workshops," added Julia.

Charlie thought that she must come from an odd family: what a crazy idea, being chaperoned at her age, in the 21st century! On the off chance that she'd accept, he ventured a new invitation.

"Later, then, after you've eaten? You could call me and I'll meet you in the lobby of my hotel. It's the same one where the gathering was held. Coffee and dessert. How about that?"

Julia hesitated but her friend gently nudged her, encouraging her to agree.

"That's perfect! See you later, say around 9 o'clock tonight?"

The door to the Lakota's libidinous plan had finally opening a crack. This woman was becoming more desirable by the minute, and her lips looked so much like Paula's, reminding him of his wife who had left to go north.

I have to ask her what Nation she belongs to, thought the shaman. *I'd bet my life she's Cree like Paula. The features of those women have a softness all their own.*

He clasped his hands in front of his erection to hide it from view. Not one easily deceived, Hélène winked knowingly at him and led Julia toward the exit.

Stretched out on the bed, flooded with desire, Charlie stared at the phone. "Is that damn thing ever going to ring?" The time they'd set had come and gone, and the world was cloaked in the black of night. The sound of the telephone startled him. Julia's youthful voice seemed to be teasing him.

"I'm here, waiting for you in the lobby!"

This time she was dressed in a blouse and jeans.

The girl travels with her entire wardrobe, thought the Sioux.

Not the least bit apologetic for her late arrival, she described how she had followed Louis and Hélène to the base of Mount Lemmon, after their meal.

"We heard rattlesnakes shaking their tails in the bushes. It was so exciting! Tomorrow morning, we're going to leave really early and hike up to the top. We'll have plenty of time since the workshops don't start until 10. The desert is fascinating! So different from my country with its lakes and huge forests! So, where are we going for dessert?"

The man was practically reeling from fatigue and impatience in the face of the beautiful girl's chatter. He asked her to follow him and headed down the hallway leading to his room.

"Come..." he said gently when she stopped in front of the open door.

Docilely, she obeyed, but remained standing in the middle of the room, uncertain and clearly nervous, hugging her purse to her chest and staring at Charlie like a deer caught in the headlights. He sat on the bed and extended a hand toward her, his expression pleading. She shook her head.

"I thought you wanted to have coffee and talk with me! What are we doing in your room? What do you want from me?" she asked in a trembling voice.

The shaman couldn't make sense of anything. All he heard was the rhythm of his heart charging through him like a wild horse, and the waves of blood crashing against the inside of his skull like the ocean's surf smashing against the cliff barring its way.

"I want you, I want to make love with you…"

Elbows on his knees, he held his head and sighed. The woman could rest assured, this giant of a man would not subject her to violence, but she was so disappointed that she couldn't stop herself from saying, "Louis and Hélène warned me. But I defended you, thinking that a medicine man like you would never think of committing acts that run counter to your mission. Boy, am I ever naïve!"

"But I'm a man!" he blurted in exasperation. "A man above all else! I'm no priest! I'm married and have a family! You think it's thanks to the Great Spirit that my wife had those kids?"

Julia was dumbfounded. Anger gave her the courage to shout, despite the late hour and the people sleeping in neighbouring rooms. "So you take advantage of these meetings to cheat on your wife? I'm going back to my hotel. I've had just about enough of this and I'm exhausted!"

She marched toward the door and was about to open it when the man realized that she was planning to walk the streets of Tucson alone at night.

"Wait! At least let me walk you back, it'll be safer for you, that's for sure…"

Charlie practically had tears in his eyes and his voice grew husky because he was sincere and believed that the Métis woman had deciphered his intentions. He knew that she was unfamiliar with the customs of his people, for whom woman is sacred, and that making love to her would be an homage to the Mother Earth that she embodied. Although he knew that she was the type who idealized shamans but forgot that they were men like all the rest, sensitive to the beauty of women,

Charlie thought that he could still persuade her. They walked peacefully down the well-lit street, and the Sioux told her of his solitude, his work, and his attraction to her, which stemmed from her resemblance to Paula, his absent wife. He felt her softening and hoped that perhaps tomorrow, after a night of reflection, she would agree to share his bed.

As they neared the hotel, she took his hand. "Charlie, thank you for telling me about yourself. I like you a lot, but I'm in love with my boyfriend, who stayed back home, at my house, and I'm not interested in having an affair."

They had nothing more to say to each other. There was an uncomfortable silence, broken by Julia, who extended Charlie an incongruous invitation.

"Would you like to meet my brother? I'm sure he's still awake since he must be waiting for me to get back."

The Lakota shaman drifted along. He stopped thinking entirely and, like a mechanical puppet, followed the woman to the elevator.

NEKA

Naomi Fontaine
Innu from Uashat

Sitting beside her, I casually take her hand. It's veiny, brown, small and gentle. I look at my own, which would be almost identical to hers if I didn't paint my nails with deep purple polish. And if my palms were smoother. Maybe time softens skin, the way age softens the look in someone's eyes.

❧

My mother doesn't talk much about her childhood. When she does, it's always about the meals. She says, "There were no vegetables, no fruit, we ate noodles all the time. I used to go to my older sister's place to drink cow's milk, we didn't have any at home." She says "cow's milk" and it makes me laugh. I wouldn't dare ask what kind of milk she drank at her house. She finds it amusing. Sort of the same way I find having had to wear my sisters' hand-me-downs laughable. It won't kill you.

I try to imagine what this reserve looked like. A poor village, inhabited by poor people, who survived on sacks of potatoes and flour. How she must have felt when she had to sleep with her sisters, three in a bed. The minuscule assortment of flower-patterned dishes, little plates and a teapot, reappearing at Christmas, year after year, the cherished artifacts from her youth.

Her father worked hard for the city, building new infra-structures. For a meager wage, as meager as the slices of meat that he alone ate when the family sat down for supper. This man of few words, my grandfather, had seen the draconian changes in his community. Like all the others of his genera-tion, he had settled his brood in a modest wood cabin. He then made up his mind that he would not moulder away in his makeshift shelter. Resilient, he did his 40 hours a week. He told his daughters to go to school, even though he could nei-ther read nor write. And although he couldn't give them steak to eat very often, no one would ever go hungry.

He was a visionary, a man capable of understanding the path his world was taking and chose to follow it.

⁂

In the boxes piled up at the back of my mother's closet, I find an Indian outfit, straight out of an old western. There's a leather vest. The artisan had embroidered an owl on the back and adorned the front with fringe. The skirt, made of match-ing fabric, looked more like a Hawaiian hula skirt with its layers of fringe than the skirts worn by our ancestors, had they actually worn skirts, those Amazons whom I pictured as being as strong as men.

"My mother had sewn for us, for my twin and me, tradi-tional clothes to wear when we started high school," she explains. "We went to the White people's school. Can you imagine how ashamed I was to wear that outfit? Dead. I'd rather have been dead."

Years later, during my last year of high school, a show had been planned as part of a fundraising campaign for the school I was attending. I offered to participate. I was going to do a tra-ditional dance to a popular Innu song. And I chose that very costume for my performance. I had added little bits of metal to the fringes on the skirt. With each step, you could hear a soft jingling that caught everyone's attention. I swanned around, my flushed cheeks burning, thrilled to have everyone's eyes on me.

❧

It's impossible to imagine my mother without her faith. I was very young when I learned what faith was: believing in something you do not see. We were little, so we followed her into this church that looked more like a community hall than a sacred place, with neither bell tower nor statues. A modern cement building next to a bowling alley, it had small windows on the sides but no stained glass. It did have a big wooden door to welcome the believers, who arrived on Sunday, wearing their finest attire, a Bible in hand.

Many memories spill from those doors. The people sang loudly, clapping their hands and smiling broadly. They knelt, they implored. They raised their hands to the heavens and were sometimes moved to tears.

Admitting to being a member of the Protestant church had created a total scandal in the family and on the reserve.

Since colonization and the missionaries, and despite the boarding schools, in our villages, it was all about the Catholic religion. Since the Innu were very spiritual beings and likely to believe in things beyond their perception, they did not find Catholicism distasteful. Suffering the misery of famines and arid winters and exhausted from battling the forest, they had accepted the idea that there was a higher power. My mother was the first to rebel, the first not to have her children baptized. The first to stay away from religious ceremonies, first communions, novenas and recitations of the rosary. She was not yet 20. She hadn't been tortured, at least not physically.

47

There is an Innu word for Protestants like my mother. They're called *kamatau-aiamiat*: those who pray in a strange way. You have to understand the rejection, the exclusion that comes of not belonging to the majority's religion. It was an insult in the eyes of a very observant people. I can't talk about her without talking about her fearlessness.

Faith is something that I have. Believing in something beyond what my eyes can see. Especially when I'm sad, especially when I'm fragile, especially when I fail to understand this unjust, cruel life that spares criminals but scorns peace-loving mothers. I believe that there is something greater than this life, but if I'm wrong and everything that exists can be seen, at least throughout my life, I'll have had hope.

～※～

Her decision to leave the reserve had surprised me one spring. We were so young, scarcely old enough to handle our boredom in the back of the big, garish green Aerostar, but we tried our best to keep still for the interminable 10-hour drive from Uashat to Québec City. We laughed ourselves silly that day, until our jaws ached, until my mother got annoyed and threatened to stop the van by the side of the road and punish us severely.

Was she escaping? Expressing a desire long repressed? Was it the culmination of a process undertaken some years earlier? Or the tentative hope that things would be better somewhere else?

I often asked myself that question. Why go so far away, when everything that belonged to us could be found in Uashat? She enrolled me in a private high school, one of the most prestigious in the city, because I'd received good grades in elementary school. Fine, except that no one had prepared me for that environment.

My friends' fathers were lawyers, professors, company presidents. My own father had foolishly died in a car accident. I was out of my league. Their mothers supervised their household and their children's schoolwork. I pictured them as very chic women, sipping a cup of hot tea as they waited for their guests in the living room. They cooked shark with tartar sauce for dinner and folded the laundry. Such women did not laugh uproariously, they crossed their legs at the knee when they sat. I did not come from the same stock. We ate shepherd's pie and macaroni with meat. Friday was fast-food night. On Sunday, we had the best meal of the week – roast chicken or steak, and mashed potatoes. There was always something for dessert.

During that whole time, between the meals and the whimsical organization of a family with five children, my mother studied. I saw her in the evening, after supper, at the huge kitchen table that she used as a desk, reading and rereading her notes from class. Closing her eyes, reciting them by heart. Memorization, I now know, serves no purpose. And so I find her single-parent reality even sadder. Like a form of torment, a hardship. It is impossible to talk about my mother without talking about her strength.

⁂

She sleeps at my place on Mondays, in my four-room apartment with bath, which overflows with toys and novels to be read. She borrows my son's room, which is in perpetual disorder. She doesn't pay it any attention. She tickles his neck, his thighs, his ribs, his back, until he squeals for her to stop. Close to tears, he begs for more, until it's time for bed. We often pray, to give thanks and ask for the courage to face another day.

Late at night, a cup of hot water in her hand, we sit like two close friends and she tells me about her work as advocate at the Uauitshitun health and social services centre. For several years, she has spent her time meeting young people, the older ones and the not-so-old. These are the defeated, the broken, those close to collapse. Their faces bear witness to a heavy, unassuaged sorrow. Completely overwhelmed, they show up one Monday, with a tiny glimmer of hope. She sees them at the very beginning of their recovery. This woman – who became a mother very young, who lived with her big brood of kids in a house provided by the Council, who was worn down by problems with money and men – this woman is the ear that listens, counsels, tries to understand, once a week, offering a helping hand in the form of a coffee.

※

One winter evening, she is exhausted. She cries. My mother's tears, as rare as they are unbearable, reminded me of a child's. Big tears, held back for so long, slide down her cheeks, and her weeping dissolves into the silence of my apartment. Awkwardly, I put a hand on her arm and she immediately pulls it away. She does not want to be consoled; she just needs to let it out, to give free rein to her immense sorrow. At last, she tells me, "I know they don't trust me. My colleagues. They look at me with suspicion, as if I wanted to harm them. And that, my girl, is the worst thing of all."

I understand only too well that feeling, as old as the hills, of not measuring up. It's not that she does not want, it's that she wants for everyone. Her years of exile taught her a certain discipline. Being able to count only on herself, she created herself out of the sacred bonds of single parenthood. She fought, and she will continue to fight throughout her life. A mother bear.

※

A few weeks later, she tells me that she has enrolled in a Master's program. I'm surprised, since I'd always thought of her as an unconventional woman. She'd been working just a few short years in a field that seemed to enthrall her, judging from the projects that she organized and to which she was deeply committed. Then, with no feeling other than that her work was done, she decided to study other things that, at first glance, seemed unnecessary but that would apparently take her further, higher. While most people walk, stagnate, wander around in circles, I had the impression that she was running. Running toward herself.

As an adult, caught between a rock and a hard place, I strive to be a woman, with all my faults, transgressions and penchants for futile endeavours. But also with the simple dignity that comes of being this woman's daughter.

⁂

That's where I fell asleep the first time, Neka. Round head, fists like two big marbles. Eyes closed. Your skin as soft and sweet as water. Mine all red and swollen. Barely enough breath to cry. Only the desire to snuggle up close. That's where I slept, between the hollow of your shoulder and the heat of your chest.

SNOWY OWL

ALYSSA JÉRÔME
Innu from Uashat Mak Mani-Utenam

Day 1. Midnight. The famous countdown is already over, the selfish glasses of bubbly are on hand for the adults, and hurried kisses invade customary personal spaces. Shimmering confetti of all colours waltz through everyone's excitement and the depleted supply of fresh air.

Everyone extends wishes for a happy new year. Will it come wearing that arousing perfume? Sadly, I do not know. My grandmother is eagerly awaiting the day when I'll introduce her to the lucky winner of my affections. She hopes he'll be Innu. My mother, on the other hand, is convinced that this Prince Charming will be as white as snow. How ironic!

The exchange of kisses and the glad-handing come to an end, and the wood floor is clogged by the crush of humanity.

I am alone. No one is laughing at my extra weight anymore. No one is talking about how little I know of my culture. I no longer feel intangible. My eyelids slowly close, my face turns toward the ceiling, my fingers gently trace the length of my neck, and I exhale all the sorrow and rage that I had to suppress for them. I lower my head. I open my eyes and stare at the ground. I bite my nails, realizing that the only person who can save my life is me.

It wasn't so long ago that I met my true self. As time went on, people passed by but never stopped when they came to me. So shoulders slouching, legs crossed, eyes downcast, and hair hiding me completely, I would sigh in nascent despair. And that's when I saw her, so dazzling under her elegant blanket, not a care in the world, so full of goodwill that they called her perverse and strength incarnate. She was the first to come see me. What is it they say about firsts? That you never forget them.

Outside, stray dogs roam, drunks frighten people, and our Innu teenagers exchange insults. Do you know their stories? Do you know the truth? I'd love to say that the dogs are just roaming free and that they go home when they're good and ready, that the abusers are just victims of an insistent injustice and that the youngsters are only trying to understand themselves. But in the big city, we know that among those mangy animals there are truly some that no longer have a home, that those drunks actually chose to make nothing of their lives, and that those kids are nothing but spoiled brats whose parents will never pay them any attention.

The old folks ask me to close the curtain. It's just before dawn and we are still awake, defiant in the face of a post-celebration silence. They've turned off the lights, and only the waves on the beach down the hill echo melodiously through the village.

I dream. I dream of fairy-tale world – a world where everyone smiles, where a captivating delight prevails. There's no prejudice. Evil doesn't exist. Lying doesn't exist. Loyalty does. No jealousy, no thieving. A sense of kinship. A people reunited. A perfect world. A world too unattainable...

Day 6. Nine a.m. I sit on a wooden bench and struggle to keep my heavy eyelids open. But I did try to make my sleepy face a bit more promising with some concealer, a few strokes of black mascara and a little red lipstick. Nothing too extravagant, compared to the other girls at this school.

While the sun was apologizing for having left us like a negligent parent, I haunted social networks like an orphan. I never thought that the stuff people rushed to share on those overused interfaces showed us who they really are. The Internet will show you a girl who spends her weekends drinking and partying with older boys, and yet she's at the top of her class and hopes to become a psychologist.

Suddenly I'm embarrassed. I have the feeling that the great star is beating down on me and that panic rules me like an absolute monarchy. She's come back under her black cloak to speak to me. I shouldn't go back to class. I know the story. I know that my confidence will hightail it off to Afghanistan and cruel comments will massacre my self-esteem. Not so long ago I was unaware that intimidation was a real thing, and then one day I knew all its synonyms. Racism. People at school think that they're not hurting anyone but, in fact, they mock my origins, my family, me. Why do they think it's charming when an English person speaks French but ridicule the attempts of an Innu who's been forced to speak their language? There are some who don't want to lose their French language and then we learn in history that the British "Blues" were the good guys. But in real life, all of them do their best to humiliate the ones who just want to make friends; they're trying to eradicate a culture that wouldn't hurt a soul.

Only five minutes left before the bell rings. I don't like time. We're always saying that we'd like to go back to correct our mistakes but, even if we walk backwards, time marches on. All I know about time is that it's always mean-spirited and that it steals our lives away from us.

French is my first class this morning. I'm happy because we're working on poems. Something I find fascinating, alluring. I love the French language. Its words are so tantalizing, and what they depict is inevitably admirable. I let its magic soothe me. To me, there's nothing more beautiful than that. And yet it also makes me sad. I have a good command of French, but Montagnais... my Innu language just doesn't do it for me. My friends often ask me to teach them words. The problem is that I have the right accent but the wrong language. I can't give them anything and so I'm worthless.

Day 35. Ten p.m. I am afraid. My mother once told me that it's normal for everyone to feel more fragile in February and March. It's normal because our planet is sick as a dog. As if it was suffering more than all the other days of the year, leaving us either hostile or despondent. Our souls bruise themselves against this malaise. As for me, I never know if I'm truly enraged because every time I scream, I cry.

Now I'm resting, in the foetal position. I'm scaring myself and thinking about my family. Who am I to them? If I'm not Pocahontas and I'm not Snow White, am I a creature from outer space? I don't know where I belong. It's absolutely outrageous that I'm compelled to choose between two cultures that I find equally interesting.

I dwell on the good days. The childhood that I buried because its memories only make me bitter. Once upon a time, we were rich. Once upon a time, people liked us. Once upon a time, we were happy. Enamoured of our own innocence. Today, that innocence has given way to fearfulness.

Day 120. Anxiety wants to help me understand life. She told me she was going for a walk and, dressed in her famous cloak of darkness, she finally left me alone for a moment. After all the pain she's put me through, she wants me to ponder the other evil that has hold of my compatriots and our Mother Earth. Nowadays I have the feeling that my mind has gone to a different galaxy. I no longer think. I no longer dream. The void has welcomed me in, and I watch.

The ocean. From Earth, it looks serene. We wade in from dry land because we love how it gently caresses our skin. Just then a wave of shivering and freshness comforts us. And yet the ocean cries. We throw all our junk into it, as if it were some wretchedly loathsome garbage can! Everyone pretends to be comrades-in-arms when we're actually a bunch of hypocrites.

When I study the trees, I see them as aggrieved. In the past, everyone hugged them and respected them. We shared them. These days, the trees have been abandoned, and we tear our hair out before them to learn who will get to live with them. Even though those who stupidly sever them from their destiny would have us believe that because they turn them into buildings, the trees belong to them. Their green falls ill, their perfume takes flight and their serenity cries out in sorrow. They were our friends but meanwhile we've chucked them into freighters...

Our Earth suffers for our vanity and no one notices. Our Earth is like the child of two parents suing each other for custody. This child is like the money we put in the middle of a poker table to sort out who will win it, and the money is like a whole life that we are threatening with monstrous weapons, just to be proven right.

Day 213. We're celebrating our deliverance. We dance and sing, we laugh, we embrace, we eat. My Indigenous Nation is admirable. Everyone is there. Our elders look on us with pride, our parents instruct us, our wonderful graduates joyfully sink their teeth into the moment, the way we would a cake, and our children run through our history.

One day, I had dinner with a lady. She had an endearing kindness about her. As we were enjoying our Italian food, she asked if the Innu had a rough time in school. I explained that everyone wants to succeed in life. Just because some have babies and others engulf themselves in vile fumes and quit school, it doesn't mean that they never tried to be successful. No one wants to admit that his presence on Earth is superfluous. My people, the Innu – just like all the other peoples of the world who differ from their neighbours – will never be able to assimilate into a culture that did not raise it. I'm afraid to admit that the social problems plaguing my community recur, like a genetic anomaly. Don't you see that today we have to leave our Native land only to surface in these urban centres for a few of years, and all of it in an environment where our customs go unrecognized? Our amazing graduates often completely forget that they once spoke Innu. To succeed, we have to annihilate everything we know.

I am a worthy Métis. I am proud to say that I learn all I can about my culture and that I will be magnificent when I prove my authenticity to everyone. French is sensuous and Innu is venerable. And between these two languages, a safe haven can be found. We have an extraordinary history and we should be proud of ourselves. Soon we'll be able to share the fairy tale with our children and inspire them to dream, and they will return to stand before the universe in our stead. The snowy owls will finally fly with confidence. Because if the power remains in Evil's grip, we will never manage to believe. It's time to become our dreams instead of acquiring them like thieves.

WHERE ARE YOU?

MICHEL JEAN
Innu from Mashteuiatsh

Where are you?

It's been a week since you plunged deep into the forest. It's as if it swallowed you up.

You would think me ridiculous if you could see me, missing you as I sit here before the stove in our tent. The little one is asleep in his hammock. He's bundled up well, he's warm, don't worry.

Malek will be like you: tall, calm and courageous. He already has your look in his eye and, like you, he never cries. Well, almost. This child observes the world with eyes as black as *Mashk*'s fur. Barely eight months old and he's the one who eases my worries. I'd like to have his strength and some of yours. The wind is blowing over the encampment and the forest is full of the cracking of trees that yield to its intensity. I feel as if I'm at the mercy of everything.

This morning, we went around to check the snares. When we go out, I always dress him in the outfit lined with rabbit fur, the one your mother made for him. The fur on his skin is so soft, and it seems that it calms him as well as protects him from the cold.

He's getting heavier. I like to feel him there on my back when I walk between the trees. Nestled against me this way, he remains silent. He is a child of the forest, and he instinctively knows how to act. Soon, he'll be hunting the small game instead of me. He will bring back jackrabbits and partridges while I take care of the camp, and you will go on expedition to the North. And one day, he will go with you. I'll need to have a girl with me. I don't want to stay in the tent by myself. But we have time for that.

The fire crackles and warms me. I know that I shouldn't, but I feel alone in the middle of the woods without you. And yet I lived my whole life here before I met you. I know what I have to do and that nature watches over me. We know each other, the forest and I. Perhaps I love you too much? Is that possible…loving too much? Is it possible to feel so much happiness when thinking of someone that you can't imagine life without him?

Sometimes I wonder if this is good. He who has nothing fears no one. But he who hides a treasure fears losing it.

Well, I'm going to sleep now. Thinking about all this gets me nowhere and only torments my soul.

I love you.

Where are you?

You should have been back three days ago by now. Was the hunting too good? Or not good enough? I'm jealous that you're up there. My father often took me to the Northern plain. I have seen the caribou herd. You hear it approaching from far away, like a whisper. A sea of animals that slowly moves in waves like those of Pekuakami. A forest of hearts pressed up against each other. Even the cold of the North can do nothing in the face of so much warmth.

The baby and I take shelter in our tent. It is sturdy. We set it up well last fall. The spruce poles are planted deeply and do not tremble, even in a strong wind. Tonight it smells good. I changed the carpet of fir boughs, and its fresh fragrance perfumes the entire place. The child sleeps in his hammock, and I let the heat of the stove toast the skin of my face. I listen to the forest. It is silent, at night, at this time of year. Surely I am not the only one who waits impatiently for spring.

I love you.

Where are you?

You should have been back with us a week ago already. Today I didn't stop for a minute. There is so much to do. Cut the wood. Trap. Go check on all the snares.

We're lucky there are jackrabbits these days because I haven't seen a single partridge since you left. But my traps are enough for us. My mother taught me well, and even the most cunning of animals never suspects that there, under a branch, hides a tether that will allow us to eat.

These creatures are our blessing. I thank them each day for their sacrifice. Without them, the baby would suffer, and that I could not bear. Just now, I placed rabbit bones around the camp, attached strings the way Mother did at home. "We must honour the animals' soul," she said. And she was right.

I'm sleepy. The day was long. I hope that you are warm and that you have skins with you. Some to cover you and some so that we can buy everything we'll need next year. That way, nothing will force you to go on expedition to the North.

I love you.

Where are you?

The wind blows hard and shakes the tent tonight. I have barely gone out since this morning because of the storm. When I was young, I used to enjoy nature's tantrums. They amused me. Now that I better understand how harsh the world is, I have more respect for its moods.

It's long, a whole day without going outside. Even the little one couldn't stand it anymore, and I had to console him more than once. Perhaps he sensed my uncertainty. I know, I worry too much. But you should have been here two weeks ago. Even though I know perfectly well that you are like a fish in water in the forest, I can't stop fretting.

It makes me lose my appetite. I ate just a little bit of blueberry jam mixed with bear fat on bannock. Why eat more when you expend so little energy? In any case, I have to save our reserves. Spring is here and soon we'll begin the descent to Mashteuiatsh. One can never be too careful. Especially with a baby. My mother always reminded me of that. I know, this makes you smile. We're not all as strong and confident as you, my love.

My family knew hardship. My grandfather was forced to move his clan the year of the famine. That winter, the game animals abandoned us. I don't know what we had done to deserve such a fate. It's what drove us to leave Pessamit and move to the peaceful shores of Pekuakami.

I tell myself that maybe it was God's secret plan. To bring us together, you and me.

I think you are so handsome, with your face and its refined, almost feminine, features. Your eyes with their black irises. Before, I saw hints of mystery in them. Now, I know that it is more likely shyness, restraint. Respect. And I learned to appreciate that in you.

When I became old enough to choose a companion, I did not want, like most of my friends, to take my time. Some went from one boy to another until they were sure of their selection. It's a good tradition. When you live in the forest, there is neither time nor place for disputes or regrets. Too many things to do. An Innu woman cannot allow herself the luxury of marrying the wrong man.

For a long time, my sister Marie dithered over three boys. I believe that she preferred Thomas's son because of his curious eyes and perpetual smile. She liked him a lot. But he had fun with his friends instead of completing his tasks.

So she chose Antoine, who does not speak or smile much, but who has heart. He is serious. She will be better off with him in the woods. She made the right choice.

For me, the question never came up. I always knew it would be you…provided that you would have me. You are my only love. I never wanted anyone else. Where are you tonight?

I love you.

Where are you?

This storm has been hammering us for three days. My snares are buried under a thick layer of snow. I'll find them; I'm not worried about that. I know how not to lose my traps. But it will still mean a lot of work for me.

Malek isn't causing me too much trouble. That child is the most beautiful gift you've ever given me. When I nurse him, when he suckles my breast, I can feel his heart beating against my chest. It reminds me of when you embrace me. I love feeling your heart beating against mine. Heart to heart. That's how we live.

Sometimes, when you sleep, I lay my head on you and listen to the beats under your skin, their rhythm slow and regular. It calms me. At that moment, I feel how alive you are. I hope that you are safe and warm tonight.

I love you.

Where are you?

I long for you and you're not here. I want your hands on me. I need your warm body pressed against my own. I yearn to feel the strength of your desire. I like that masculine urgency that reveals your love.

The other girls say that men are often brusque, that men hurt them and that they end up dreading their embrace. You have never hurt me. I have never been afraid of you, your hands, your mouth.

I like it when you gaze into my eyes. Between us, no words are necessary. Your hands caress me at their leisure. Your lips seek mine. You bind yourself to me with a combination of gentleness and raw strength that amazes me every time. I miss abandoning myself to your ardour.

Desire burns in my belly. And you are not here.

I love you.

Where are you?

Are you safe? Are you still alive, my love? Imagining the worst breaks my heart. I cannot imagine you other than bursting with life. It's been seven weeks since you left. I tell myself that it was foolish to let you go there alone. I should never have listened to you.

"Malek is still too fragile," you said. "I know the way and I've been there several times with my father."

Words. They're nothing but words. Insanity! Yes! It was already daring enough to spend the winter alone, just the three of us. My uncle, who is a widower, offered to come with us instead of going with my family on the Manouane. You thanked him and told him that it was your responsibility to ensure the well-being of your own family.

I found your pride romantic and touching. I had complete confidence in you. In us. But today, I think it was reckless.

I don't know this territory well. If it were the Manouane, I would know where to look. But this is your home, and I am not too sure where the trails you took to the North lead. It's a beautiful area and the river is majestic. The dense forest protects us well. There is game. But the great Northern plain is far away.

Tomorrow, if you have not returned, I will go down the river to the Gill's encampment. It's a good full day of snowshoeing from here. I will ask them to help me search for you. Old Rosaire is a wise man. He'll know what to do.

I love you.

Where are you?

I am with the Gills tonight. I will sleep here and return to the tent tomorrow. This morning, the baby and I left early. It's a long walk, but you just have to follow the river. They welcomed me warmly. His wife prepared dinner and afterward, around the fire, Rosaire Gill listened to me. He looked at me with tired but still lively eyes. He reproached me for not coming to see him sooner.

He is right. Tomorrow, his two sons will come back to the tent with me. Then they will go look for you. Old Gill knows the area, as do you. He said that you'll be found. That he's sure you let yourself be drawn away by the bountiful hunting. "It's good to collect many skins, but you have to think about returning home because it's springtime and soon the mild temperatures will make it hard to walk in the forest. Soon it will be time to leave this land and return to the banks of the Pekuakami."

His words reassured me. Being able to count on your neighbours in the woods is important. We live in isolation, each one on his share of the land, but there is always another family nearby should you need help. I was comforted by the sound of voices other than the baby's or my own. And by the sound of laughter. Even if it made me think of your laughter. Everything brings me back to you. The details of life, the memories, the smells.

I noticed that the Gills had already begun their preparations for the journey home. And that reminds me that we must soon do the same. Come back quickly because I will not leave without you, my beloved.

I love you.

Where are you?

The flights of *Nishk* have been passing over our heads for several days now. Do you see them? When I hear them

arriving from the south with their incessant honking, I immediately go out to admire the invisible wave that they draw in
the sky with their powerful wings.

This morning, an immense flock flew right over our camp,
at low altitude. There were so many birds that the sky dark-
ened, as if night had fallen, and their song was so loud that I
could hear nothing but that.

I took out my rifle and shot a big bird. Its outstretched
wings were wider than I am tall. I saved the down, the wings,
the feathers. I grilled the feet over the fire and ate them. It was
so good. My mother used to boil them but I always preferred
cooking them right over the fire. I roasted the animal as well
and ate almost all of it. It felt so good to eat something other
than our ordinary winter fare! Had you been here, we would
have made a party of it. I kept a piece for you in any case, and
I'll give it to you if you return tomorrow.

I started to put our things away. I have to keep busy until
you come back. It's already been five days since the Gill boys
left to search for you. I would have liked to go with them. But
Rosaire insisted that I stay here to care for the little one...and
in case you should come back. I can't stand this waiting for
you any longer.

All the provisions, the furs and packs must be organized
for the return trip. It will take me a few days to finish the work
by myself but I'll manage, and we'll be ready to go down with
the others when the snow has melted and the river starts to
run again.

I love you.

Where are you?

The river carried the ice away last night. I was awakened
by a crack of thunder over the water. Then, from my bed, I
heard the water flowing. The river, which we had both seen
hardening into ice and then being covered by a blanket of

snow, is now reborn. Spring is beautiful. The weather is mild and the snow produces lovely music as it melts. I will be able to fish and hunt for muskrat.

I love you.

Where are you?

I am heavy-hearted tonight. I cry but, rest assured, our child does not notice this. The Gills' sons did not find you. After spending two weeks looking for you, they had to return without you.

They saw no tracks, and I must tell you that I do not understand. No encampment. And yet I told them which trail you were planning to take. The profusion of snow must have erased your footprints. They followed them up to the Northern plain and then they found nothing but silence.

I don't know what to think anymore. I considered the possibility that you had decided to leave me. That you regretted having made a commitment to me. I am just a simple girl with nothing extraordinary about me other than my love for you. You, a man so handsome and so strong. All the girls wanted you. And I was the one you chose, the one who had always loved you.

I remember how proud I was the day we went to our land as a family – you, me and the baby. Our child, so gentle, like you.

Perhaps you got bored? Or did you perhaps change your mind? It would be your right to do so. Have you left me, my love? Did you follow the rivers to Naskapi territory? Or to Cree territory to the west?

I am in our tent. The fire keeps the two of us warm. It dries the tears that no one else sees. I changed the carpet of fir branches this morning and it fills the place with its perfume. I am in our own little nest. Hurry back to me.

I love you.

Where are you?

Darling, I killed *Mashk*! Can you believe it? Me! It was a huge male, immense. Heavy with sleep, he did not see the trap that we had placed near the clearing. The big tree trunk that I had put in position smashed his skull. I still had to finish him off with the rifle. I was as excited as a child. You should have seen me. Even the little one looked happy. He waved his arms and laughed.

I offered up a bit of tobacco to *Mashk's* soul, in his honour. Obviously, I could not pull the beast out by myself so I carved him up right there in the ditch. It took me the entire day.

I was very careful not to offend the animal's spirit. I buried his droppings under the hearth, I threw the bones into the fire and attached some of them to the trees as well.

My father often told me about *Mashk*. He told me that we owed him respect because he is the most powerful being in the forest. He is cunning and intelligent. He is the master of life and death but the Innu, said my father, must defeat him. And that is what I did. I'm so proud of myself! Your absence is the only thing keeping my happiness from being complete.

I grilled the head over the fire and I ate it. I smoke-dried the rest of the meat for three days in order to preserve it. It's a lot of work, especially with such a massive animal. But I did everything the right way. I carved the meat into thin slices. If you try to smoke big chunks, the meat will be ruined.

Then I fed the fire with damp, rotting stumps. It made a nice, thick smoke. From time to time, I added spruce boughs.

I meticulously collected the fat and put it into little birchbark containers. Spring fat isn't as good as autumn's, when *Mashk* has stuffed himself with blueberries. But it's still good.

We have provisions to last a long time. We'll be able to share with the others when we go back downriver and meet them at the Manouane fork. No one will believe that I'm the one who did all this. You will be proud of me.

I love you.

Where are you?

Today, I saw two families go down the Peribonka. They stopped to greet me. I asked if they had seen you, but they had not. Of course, they had spent winter a little east of the river. It was surely not on your route.

I told them that you would arrive soon and that we would be moving on too. "We'll see each other at the Manouane fork then," said the mother, who looked upon me with kind eyes. I understood that she shared my concern. I am not the first woman to worry about her man.

Our people have begun their descent. By this time, some of them must have already reached the spring gathering place, at the mouth of the beautiful river that flows to Lake Manouane.

My parents must be arriving soon. Their land north of the lake thaws later and they are among the last. But there the hunting and trapping are good, and my father always brings back a lot of meat. It makes for good opportunities to celebrate when we're all together again, with the first warm weather.

I enjoy life in the woods. I enjoy the relative solitude of our nomadic world, in the middle of the forest and its melodies. But come springtime, I feel the need to see the others. Each family leaves the woods and heads back along the trail that, in the fall, led to its land. Except that the trip back down goes more quickly and, more importantly, it's easier.

It took us a month to reach Passes-Dangereuses, and I'll wager that in two weeks we'll be at Mashteuiatsh. It will only take us a few more days to get to the Manouane fork.

I can't wait to see my mother and sister. And my father. This is the first winter I am spending without them and the first time I am not going up my river with its high, austere cliffs.

When I chose you, I chose your land and your Peribonka. Your forest resembles ours but the river is different. The Peribonka seems more turbulent. There are many rapids that force us to portage. But that does not frighten me. I carry my share, and soon the little one will do the same.

Thinking about all that is dear to me helps me endure the tent's silence, which is broken only by the soft, regular breathing of our child. There is no end to the emptiness inside me. When I dive into it, it feels as if I am drowning, falling into a siphon that carries me into the dark bowels of the Earth. Where are you, for the love of God? What has happened to keep you from returning to me? You promised, you swore to me! I have so much confidence in you. What has happened?

No, I don't even want to consider the possibility that you might be dead. You are strong. Full of that masculine energy I so love. You've just had a mishap.

Am I foolish to think so? Sometimes I wonder. You never would have been so late coming home. You never would have forgotten to leave a few traces behind so that we could find you. I do not understand any of this. What is holding you back? I can't take it anymore. Not knowing is unbearable.

I love you.

Where are you?

Last night, I dreamt that you were sleeping under the water. The ice had given way and you could not make it back to the surface. You had drowned and your body was lying at the bottom of a lake, in sepulchral darkness.

I hate the idea that your lungs are filled with liquid and that your open eyes stare at the invisible roof of ice above your head. That your beautiful body, which quivered under my caresses and trembled when I bared myself to you, is now no more than a frozen corpse at the bottom of a lake. That is not you. It cannot be you. You are warm, sweet, lively and tender. Not cold and stiff.

I must calm down. When I cry too much, the baby wakes up and senses my disquiet. He is like you, sensitive, and, even though he is still only a child, he wants to help me. He looks at me with his dark eyes in whose depths shines the same light that shines in yours. This eases my pain somewhat. With him, I am not utterly alone.

I am falling-down tired. I can't take it anymore. Your absence exhausts me, drains me of my life. Our life. Come back.

I love you.

Today, I left our camp. I pitched the tent on a shore of fine sand. The little one and I will sleep here tonight. I left one canoe behind, for you, if ever you return. It is well-mounted on the shelter that you built last autumn. I left provisions, too: smoked meat, bear fat and a bit of jam.

I am sitting in our travelling tent. Our baby sleeps in my arms, which struggle to hold him, so tired am I. I did two portages and one had me scaling a tall mountain with the baby on my back. I had to make two trips to carry all the supplies and the canoe.

Moving helps me forget the pain. Occupied by my tasks, I did not see the day go by and I forgot the wound that your absence has carved into my belly. Sometimes it subsides but it always returns, in the evening, when I find myself as I am now, alone before the fire that warms my face. But it can do nothing to rekindle the warmth in my ice-bound heart.

Another two days and we will be at the Manouane fork. What will the others say when they see us arriving alone? I have stopped counting how many days you have been gone because it makes me suffer so. The night is cold and I sink into the heavy *Mashk* pelt you gave me. Closing my eyes, I can almost feel your body curled up against mine and smell the musky odour of your skin.

Where are you?

THE TOMAHAWK
STRIKES A BLOW

JEAN SIOUI
Wendat Nation in Wendake

I am Thodatooan, He-Who-Speaks-with-Honour. That is what
my people named me on the day I was born. It is now August
16, 1657, according to the White man's calendar. In the
woods, the light plays between the tree stumps. The rolling
hills rise up, their feet in the warm water of summer. A light
wind carries the scent of pine trees across the trails that we
follow. For 60 days now, I have walked with 50 men and
women of my people, the brave Arendharonons, alongside a
band of warriors with panic-stricken eyes. Iroquois rebels
leading a civil war that divides us as never before. Fools who
defy the great order of the Circle. Many of them are
Onondagas and Tsonnontouans. I fought these same men
who now escort us. I saw the fury on their faces, and today I
see them jubilant. They sing and laugh, ready to help us, but
I keep seeing them under colour of war. Just a few days ago,
they killed Old Sakatia without a second thought because he
couldn't keep up with the band.

We move forward this way, each of us afraid of receiving
an arrow in the back. The French following our tracks are
quite unreliable allies. How can we trust a White man who
sneaks into the lands that the Great Spirit gave us when the
world was new? A people so unlike us, come from afar, with
linear thinking so different from our own. A civilization that

wants only to dominate us. Colonizers who see only the world right in front of them and are willing to destroy everything in their path because they worship power and riches. People who do not know that they should turn around and look back to learn from the wisdom of the Elders.

Several nights, when I was still young, I dreamt of the day when, from my hiding place under some fir branches, I saw a man – now an old insurgent among those purporting to adopt me – gasping for breath. He gave a great cry and smashed his club down on my mother's head. She collapsed as she looked at me one last time, or perhaps at my father, who lay prostrate at her side, an arrow through his neck. Last night, when the moon was full, I had a new dream in which I saw my wife, who now lives among the dead, calling to me. My wife, a woman who smelled of wild berries picked in a garden that belonged to a clan more ancient than the old oak on the hill where my ancestors now lie. A red-blooded woman, a mother who turned her children's sadness into joy. The one who taught me to dream. She appeared to me with sorrow-filled eyes and a prayer that flowed from them onto lips that stammered, "Let the noble fire of our nation's cry rekindle your heart. Take courage in the blood of our Elders."

It was a prophecy. In the morning, as soon as I opened my eyes, I understood that she had come to me to warn me that a great misfortune would befall us. I feel that our end is near, that this slow voyage through our weary silence is leading us to the painful fate that has already been spreading across our pox-ridden lands for far too long.

At day's end, after long hours spent walking, we stop to regain our strength. Suddenly, I hear someone screaming at the top of his lungs. A cry meant to gutlessly crush the confidence of men and women already ravaged by countless wars, stricken by famine in a territory destroyed by hate, and debilitated by the epidemics brought through contact with the

White man. I quickly turn around to see a young warrior, tomahawk in hand, charging toward me. I try to escape by rapidly leaning forward but he still manages to strike me, a solid blow to the right side of my head. I fall to the ground. The trees whirl around me. Blood spurts from my ears and pain takes control of my senses. My head feels detached from my body, my thoughts are buffeted by violent waves. I know this is the end of me and that I am on the path toward the land of the dead, where my parents await me. Then, in my delirium, I hear a voice that says, "Let him live, for this man once saved me."

My head hurts. It is cold and dark. Where am I now? Am I dead? I do not believe so since I feel the breeze caressing my head as it rests on a stone stained with my blood. The breath of the West Wind orders me to stand. I obey with difficulty. I am still in the same forest where I fell after the attack. What had happened? The bodies of several men lie about me. All friends, all brothers. Not one of the Wendats is left alive. Not one of our women lies next to her man for the final slumber. They must have been stripped of their goods and taken as slaves. Nor are there any Frenchmen among the dead. Instinct did well to tell me that I could not trust them. What am I to do now? I am alone in the forest, so far from the village where some, persuaded to abandon their traditions by the black cassocks and their rosaries of promises, are already battling the prolific death devastating the Savage's red blood. Why hadn't I been killed like the others? Perhaps the god Iouskeha, protector of our world, wanted me to live. But why? The pain is making my mind wander. I see my wife in ceremonial garb, dancing in the air. A brown bear licks my head wound. I stumble. I fall. I get up again. I speak to the trees. "I will lie down beneath your boughs and perhaps I will find the answers in my sleep."

The warmth wakens me. "What would we do without your strength, Great Brother Sun?" Its energy soaks into me and convinces me to get up and follow the path to my people. They are several days' walk away. I must go. I struggle to stand. Everything spins around me. Staggering, I head north toward my village. Eat, I must eat. Rebuild my strength... Move forward. Do not fall. Do not fall again. As I walk along the path, many little berries appease my hunger. I ask the same questions over and over again. What is this all about? What happened? Then my thoughts take me back to my childhood. The reasons for this carnage are long-standing. In this difficult time that pierces my heart, I remember Old Ochastegin's prophesy.

It was the season of ice. Our allies, the Onontchataronons, came to spend the winter with us, as was the custom. They talked incessantly of these White men called the French. I remember seeing Ochastegin, the Arendharonons' peace chief, sitting beside the Great River one evening. He was praying to the Moon Spirit to allay his fears. He sensed something that he could not explain. From his position on a rock, he stared at the horizon. The water, the ice, the waves, and the biting wind numbed him as his mind drifted through old thoughts. Omens that announced the arrival of strange men with ways that differed from our own. In a dream, he envisioned the appearance of a ship like none he'd ever seen. The sailors dropped anchor. A White man with an enormous hat jumped into a smaller boat and came ashore. He waved a hand and came to talk to Ochastegin. Ochastegin remained motionless as he listened to the man utter words he did not understand. But in his heart, he heard the Spirits tell him that life would never be the same again in the Land of the Rising Sun. Once back in our longhouse, he told me, "One day, young warrior, you will have to conduct our affairs with men who do not respect the order of the Circle." In this Ancestor's wrinkled face glowed eyes full of kindness. Eyes that expressed love, sharing and respect. Such was the wisdom of Ochastegin, the wisdom of my people.

I now understand what he wanted to teach me. Alone on the trail, on my way to those I miss so much, I reconsider Ochastegin's prophecy. I weep over the tribulations of my people. No more than a handful of Wendats have survived the ravages caused by the invaders. I now understand the betrayal of these Iroquoians. Several, who were like brothers to me, did not want to engage in deliberations to preserve the peace. Those barren hearts managed to persuade us, just 50 Wendats, to go live among them with the assurance that no harm would come to us. During my long trek, I remind myself what happened to us. Then just before the snowy season, exhausted and emaciated even though nature provided enough to keep me from dying of hunger, I finally reach my destination.

A Wendat Nation Council of Chiefs and Elders meets around a great fire. I sit with them and tell them what my group had gone through: the agreement with the Iroquois, the French who escorted us...the massacre.

The next day at sunrise, I go with the chiefs to see the French governor and request his help, a kind of help quite different from any that had previously been offered. It is I, Thodatooan, He-Who-Speaks-with-Honour, who converses with the governor at his fort. I recount what has happened since the Whites arrived on our lands and how my people have gone from being so strong to so weak in less than 50 years. In an impassioned speech that explains the fragility of life and the refusal to accept death, I tell the man wearing gloves that the Wendat Nation will never disappear from the back of the Great Turtle. Here where Ataensic, the woman who came down from the sky, our Mother, created the world. The "men with long eyebrows," as the village children call the strangers, must forge a just alliance with the Savages in the hope of working together to navigate the country's endless river.

We quickly learned that while the French preachify and dance the minuet, the English do business. They fight and take control of the country a few years later. It is with the conquerors that the Huron-Wendats and the steel-eyed governor from a fog-shrouded land, head of the British troops, meet face to face to conclude a treaty restoring order to the land. I, Thodatooan, He-Who-Speaks-with-Honour, witnessed the signing of this unlimited treaty that affirms our freedom of trade and of religion, and our right to practice our customs: hunting, fishing, trapping, and gathering. A treaty that protects our traditional ceremonies and ensures us the peaceful enjoyment of our territory.

Today, after a long voyage, I rest in the land of souls, where I have rejoined my wife, my parents, and my ancestors. I am at peace among the Braves after having established the legacy of a strong and powerful nation for seven generations to come. I leave to them the story of the Huron-Wendats, which gathers memories together so that never again shall come a night that seeks an end to our existence.

MITATAMUN MEANS REGRET

MAYA COUSINEAU-MOLLEN
Innu from Ekuanitshit (Mingan)

The first thing Anish did when she turned on her cell phone was check to see who had looked at her profile. She gave an exasperated sigh as she read the last message she'd received on the dating site that one of her girlfriends had recommended. Being single after a stormy relationship was far from easy. After a decade as part of a couple, finding herself back on the market required a period of adjustment that she hadn't always appreciated. Especially with all the new advances in technology that gave her more headaches than did the rare little benders she engaged in with her girlfriend.

Anish was tall and athletic, and she could pass as Chinese, Japanese or even Spanish. Her Native ancestry, once revealed, earned her her share of offers of reasonable accommodations. She had read all kinds of them, from the classic Pocahontas fantasy, which occasionally came with the option to wear little fringed buckskins, to the comment "I've never done it with a real Indian," which she classified under the categories "test drive" and "world-class asshole." Anish no longer knew where to put her trust to find love again.

To take her mind off things, she decided to hop in the car and do her thinking at the mall. Walking through the boutiques without looking for anything in particular lightened her mood even if it sometimes loaded her credit card. She made the mistake of going into her favourite shoe store where she came upon a pair of turquoise sandals set with orange and dark turquoise glass beads. She instantly saw herself walking in the sun with those beauties on her feet. All smiles, the salesgirl provided the ultimate argument: they were on sale. So Anish headed to the cash register, followed closely by a woman also intent on completing her purchases.

Anish hesitated a moment before handing her Indian status card to the cashier. For once, the young salesgirl didn't make a fuss, although she didn't remember the proper procedure. She called her manager over and said, "Hey, Céline, I forget if it's F4 or F5 to take off the 5% federal tax!"

Anish was mortified and wished she could disappear. Then the lady behind her asked, "Oh, is there a discount today?"

The salesgirl looked embarrassed and answered, "No, it's just for this lady, she has an Indian card..."

The client's retort had a slightly mocking tone. "So if I have an Italian card, can I get the taxes off too?"

Anish wavered between leaving, bathed in shame, without the sandals, and replying.

She turned to the client and said, "Ma'am, this card of mine, which makes me an 'Indian,' comes from assimilationist policies set by Canadian bureaucrats. They put us on reserves before denying us the right to move around freely. Oh, and yes, I forgot, they also took away our right to vote because that was reserved only for taxpayers. Even today, we're treated like wards of the State. And now I have this card that defines my identity."

The client took a few seconds before she answered in a lowered voice, "You're right, ma'am."

Surprised, Anish, gave her a quick smile and paid for the sandals. She had an odd feeling as she left the boutique, a mixture of uneasiness and accomplishment. Her life as a Native caused her to suffer, torn as she was between the unconditional love of her French-Canadian family and the bigotry she endured outside of her family circle. It felt as if she was bearing a sociopolitical weight on her shoulders, a burden she considered too great to bear. She took her status card out again to look at it. She stared off into the distance and made a somewhat impulsive decision.

Anish left the tattoo parlour, grimacing in pain. She'd sworn never to get inked but after the events of Idle No More, her thoughts on the subject had changed. The tattoo was not a flower or a feather, and certainly not an arrow, nothing typically "Indian." Her neck would henceforth bear a bar code and the numbers 099 00555 02. To most people, the numbers made no sense, but to the trained eye of a Native, it appeared to be a band number.

As she entered the café, Anish didn't see that a friend was right behind her. Meryl's eyes widened at the sight of the tattooed neck and she startled Anish by placing a hand on her shoulder.

"Hi, Anish! Uh, what's that on your neck? I hope it's only temporary!"

Anish looked at her friend and said, "I wanted be something of an activist so I had my band number tattooed on my neck. It's a symbol of protest. It's like the numbers tattooed on the Jews during the Holocaust."

Meryl sighed and smiled at her indulgently. "You're going to look like a convict getting out of prison."

Anish shrugged her shoulders and replied, "Oh, y'know, being an Indian in this country is a bit like being locked up in jail."

The plane flew over the river. As usual, the change of air in the cabin had knocked Anish out, and she had slept through most of the flight. She woke up slowly and thought about how much she enjoyed the time she spent at the airport.

She considered it a place open to thousands of possibilities. She loved the hours spent in the air and the mad dash from one terminal to another. It was a change from little towns where people, recognizing her origins, threw shade at her. Sometimes it was crudely obvious; sometimes it was the hypocritical subtlety in a slightly envious comment on the privileges enjoyed by Indians living on the reserves.

Over the years, she'd had to learn to control herself since she was prone to quick reactions, but she occasionally liked to give herself a pass, snapping at a narrow-minded oaf who wasn't expecting the virulence of her comment on the flagrant lack of culture afflicting the poor soul. She always felt a dull anger eating away at her. She did, however, have a circle of level-headed friends who let her vent her frustrations.

But sometimes, high above the clouds, in the imagined neutrality that the airplane provided between the sky and herself, a tiny tear spilled from the corner of her dark, almond-shaped eye.

Since she had grown up among White people, the members of the opposite sex that appealed to her naturally tended to be of that same hue. She remembered one encounter and it still resonated within her with all the brutality of the moment. He crossed the road, dressed simply, hair dishevelled and his ever-anxious eyes searching for her in the hotel lobby. His name was Luke and he was trying to find a way to escape his hasty marriage, which was condemning him to a life of sexual frustration.

Luke and Anish had met for the first time in the pixelated universe of anonymous dating-site introductions. Anish, hurt by her last relationship, was looking only for what the magazines called a "friend with benefits." She no longer wanted to make a commitment nor, in particular, did she want to fall in love. A desire for pleasures of the flesh and satisfaction of the senses motivated her search. She told herself that dating sites would not only help her find that rare bird but also breathe new life into the joys of written correspondence. True, pen and ink had been replaced by a keyboard and a frigid screen, but at least she could take her time sorting out the jerks, perverts, exhibitionists, racists, and suck-ups. When she described her difficulties to her best friend, they laughed a lot but also found the prospects somewhat bleak.

When Luke had registered on the site, he had done so after a long period of soul-searching. Without trying to justify anything, he recalled all the gestures and kindnesses he had offered his wife in an effort to rekindle their passion. There had been dinners, gifts, flowers, love notes, and romantic weekends, but still he ran up against an iciness that was both corporal and communicational. He had certainly had his share of temptations and failed attempts with other young women, but he hadn't managed to take the plunge.

After a year of involuntary abstinence, he had to choose between divorcing, which would destroy his family, and yielding to the urge to find a mistress who could satisfy his desires. He had decided upon the latter. Anish's profile was straightforward and he liked the photos she had posted. He wondered about her ethnic background. He hesitated between Japanese and Mexican. He had clicked on the icon to send a message and had written: "Hello. I really like your profile. Take a look at mine. It explains my situation very well. Let me know if you're interested."

When Anish had received the message, she had taken the time to read it and then went to check out the profile of this new breed of bonehead. She had cracked her knuckles like someone preparing to write a scathing review, but she had hesitated and looked at his picture. He had finely drawn features, his eyes were big and brown, and his lips curled into a smile. There was something about the way he looked at the camera that had made her answer this: "Hi, yes, I read your profile... I don't know what to say, I'm not sure we're really after the same thing. To be honest, I'm not sure I'm comfortable with the idea of a married man."

The answer had appeared on Luke's screen and he told himself that he should just go for broke. "Let me reassure you right up front, I'm not looking for a lover. I'd like to meet someone I can have a good time with. As I said in my profile, I rarely make love with my wife. We don't have the same needs when it comes to that. I'm not looking to ruin my family, I just want to find elsewhere what I don't have at home. I really like your photos, you have a nice smile and I was wondering what your ancestry is..."

Anish had read this message with a wry smile.

"I'm First Nations. Thanks for the compliments. And you, are you French-Canadian?"

Luke had written back just as quickly: "Yeah, a real dyed-in-the-wool Quebecker. I'm really happy you're Native. You're the first one I've talked to!"

Anish had raised her eyes to the heavens: this had "Indian lover" written all over it. Yet he appealed to her. Considering what she was looking for, she would have to find her potential lover attractive, at least at the outset. Thus had begun the long virtual discussions between Luke and Anish. They had chatted about this and that and, after about a month, they had finally decided it was time to meet. Luke had succeeded in winning her over, which had not been easy to do at first, especially when he wanted to draw her into conversations about sexuality and fantasies. Although Anish claimed she was open-minded, she realized that she had built a barrier between her needs and the possibility of satisfying them. Luke was patient and broad-minded as well as quite bold, which unnerved her but made her smile nonetheless.

When the date had been set and the hotel found, Anish had butterflies in her stomach but hadn't really asked herself why. She had chalked it up to the excitement of the moment.

When the encounter had taken place, Anish had not felt the sly jolt of love at first sight strike her very heart. Afterward, she had written a somewhat sappy text to keep a more vivid memory alive. She opened the file saved on her computer and read it again. A full year had passed since this transformative episode had occurred.

I saw him walking down the street. I started to feel more nervous and I began to make somewhat sudden movements. I liked the simple, relaxed way he was dressed, nothing pretentious.

He crossed the threshold, just as I did, psychologically speaking. Tall and thin, with the big brown eyes that I found so attractive in his picture. The first exchanges where embarrassment was apparent in everything we did and said. I wonder what he thought of me when he saw me. Did I meet his criteria? Would he want me the same way he did during our conversations online? Would he just take what he needed and then leave, like the shooting stars we attach our foolish wishes to?

There were silences and I looked him in the eye. How do you tell a man that you want him and that you want to take things a step further? It was quick and a bit hazy.

In such moments of first contact, I have all the elegance of a penguin bathing in mud… I'm shy and awkward. I was wearing high heels and almost fell. That'll teach me.

As we sat like two schoolchildren caught misbehaving, our words floated about the room. My lips closed in on his neck and his perfectly shaped ear. I caressed him and kissed his neck behind the ear, I heard him moan and breathe more heavily, my hand rose toward his neck and we kissed. The softness of his mouth on mine left me feeling a way that I had long forgotten I could feel. When he grabbed me by the hair, I caught the hungry look in his eyes. That's the look I wanted. In his photo, he smiled sincerely, careful to make a good impression. I wanted to see this man turned on, thirsting for more. His kisses grew more passionate and I, more and more aroused. He used his mouth to good effect and his tongue proved he was an expert in the art of subduing his prey, leaving her compliant and gasping for breath.

He began to fondle my breast and kiss my neck. With all the clumsiness of a first time, we managed to undress. This part is fairly vague, but I do remember the flood of sensations and desires that overwhelmed us in that moment. Our kisses, the looks exchanged, our bodies intertwined, the few words spoken.

He bit my shoulders with the fervour of a starving man. I heard myself moan with the pain that quickly turned to shameless pleasure. He had forbidden me to leave a mark on him, which was very frustrating. In a voice altered by desire, he asked if he could touch me between my thighs. The feeling of his mouth, his tongue on my sex made me groan with delight. His hand clasped mine and we found each other together again after centuries of searching, and just as quickly lost each other again.

As I wander through my memories, I know that I gave him pleasure. He felt good and tender, and he awakened my dormant sensuality, which sought to return his caresses and embraces. There was a moment of awkwardness when he was lying above me, between my legs, and I rose up toward him and looked him full in the face. He found it intimidating. I was looking at him because I liked feeling his eyes on me. I allowed myself to touch his face, the bridge of his nose, his forehead. I told him the little fantasies that are only revealed in the shared space of a certain intimacy. That must have relit the flame because he wrapped me in his arms and took me. I moaned with excitement. I wanted to feel him inside me; I wanted him to possess me. He kissed me and I only wanted more. At the very moment when pleasure reached its peak, he grabbed my arms and held them above my head, *whispering, "You like fucking a married man, don't cha." I said yes.*

Anish blushed a bit as she reread her words. But at least writing them had set her free. Their encounters had gone on for many months, but Anish's sixth sense began to stir when she felt slight hesitations on his part. She had calmly accepted the circumstances of this relationship. She had tried to maintain a distance between them, but with a delicate comment here and a well-timed compliment there, Luke had slowly but surely broken through the young woman's defences. Then came the dreaded email from her lover. It held all the doubts and fears of this man who had taken on such importance in her life and in her thoughts. He wrote that he was no longer sure that he wanted to continue their relationship. He was asking himself a lot of questions about his marriage and was finding it harder and harder to live with his conscience. He promised Anish that he would have fond memories of her and that he might write a song inspired by their relationship. Luke was a man with an artist's temperament who refused to live life to the fullest and who tailored himself to social norms.

Anish continued reading what she'd written about the experience with Luke. She wearily remembered how hard the days following the end of their liaison had been.

You'd like this welcoming house, so open and full of poetry. It would tenderly touch your sensibilities. You'd be inspired to write new songs here. It smells wonderful, like a Spanish inn.

I was listening to that haunting song by Pierre Lapointe, Les Délicieux Amants. That damn song that should be heard on a night with a full moon and a glass of vodka. And like Pierre, I wonder if you still think about me on those nights when you can't sleep…or when you feel all-powerful, your prey caught between your teeth. And here I am, alone again, wondering if the gods were angry with me…

I suffer from your absence. I cling to the lyrics I heard last night. I picture your big eyes, how telling they are. I see your face, like a tormented archangel's, when you were in that room, seeming to want me and battling your conscience. You had the look of a man who aims to please, asking me if I liked your new haircut. I wanted so badly to feel your hands on me, and tears burn down my cheeks when I remember your sign of rejection and how you backed away from me when I wanted to embrace you, as if you were refusing to let me defile you.

My only request was that you kiss me, so that I could see you approach to brush my lips with yours, to know the taste that made a slave of me. But even with that, your manner was reserved, you controlled yourself and refrained from speaking, as you know how to do so well. I remember the intensity in your eyes, filled as they were with desire. And all the while you punished yourself and donned a hair shirt to deny the pleasures of the flesh.

The pain I felt froze my cells because I saw the last minutes approaching. You wanted me to take those few steps with you along that paltry distance while I preferred to stay by the window, to be close to the void into which I wanted to let myself fall. When you finally took me in your arms, did you feel me trying to distance myself? I quickly learn to control my actions when I'm being rejected.

You left and the room shrunk to insignificance. I felt myself dying and struggling for air. As Gaston Miron says in his poem Je t'écris: *"Moi j'ai noir éclaté dans la tête." Blackness bursting in my head, yes, that is how I felt. My tears carved their path to liberty, betraying me – the one who did not want to fall, who did want to be seduced. Who wanted only the physicality of your body and not the beauty of your soul. You entered into my innermost self with your passion, into the heart of this woodland girl, into the soul of this woman who would prefer to remain the lover of liberty...*

Anish gently closed her computer. This chapter of her love life had taught her that this kind of passion existed but not without its cost. Anish's plane landed at the little airport in the North Shore city. She had little luggage so it didn't take her long to jump into a taxi.

A gloomy Wednesday was coming to an end in the grey city. Anish and her mother, Hélène, strolled up and down the aisles of the big box store. Her mother was an old woman and wore her salt-and-pepper hair with dignity, but her face said that she was worn out by the constant suffering she endured in silence. Her French-Canadian accent and the pallor of her skin stood in sharp contrast to her companion's almond-shaped eyes and black hair. Hélène was finishing her errands.

As they walked along the shelves of spices, odours of cinnamon and nutmeg tickled their noses. Hélène wrinkled hers and sneezed. She leaned on Anish's arm, which earned them a couple's curious look. The old lady's gesture demonstrated a familiarity that only a mother or a close friend or relative would be allowed to show. The pair wondered if the young woman was a caregiver, but their long shopping list made them quickly forget this pointless line of questioning.

Anish took a tissue out of her jacket and offered it to Hélène, who leaned on her shopping cart to blow her nose. She asked Anish, "Would you like to stop for lunch, dear? I'm tired and must sit down, my back is killing me."

"Sure, Mom. Shall I push the cart to the counter for you?"

"No, no," said her mother. "You know I like to lean on it. It makes it easier for me to walk."

When they reached the lunch counter, they each ordered a hot dog. Once seated, Hélène attacked her meal with obvious enthusiasm. Anish watched her eat with both fondness and amusement.

Suddenly, Hélène put down her hot dog and stroked her daughter's hand. From the corner of her eye, she caught the reaction of the elderly couple sitting next to her. She had never quite gotten used to these occasionally inappropriate reactions or gestures. When she had decided to adopt the young woman, she had never asked questions about the colour of her skin or her ethnicity. Hélène had grown up not far from an Indian reserve, as they were called back in the day. She had always found these mysterious people intelligent and the way they expressed themselves fascinating, with their laugh-loving faces bronzed and burnished by the north wind and the cold that descended from the tundra. She thought of the Innu women who had come to see her mother to ask for help delivering their babies. Hélène also remembered the distance from the people in neighbouring villages, who called her and her sisters "squaws." Her most poignant memory was of the day Anish's mother had asked her to adopt her daughter.

It had happened in December, a joyful, family-oriented month when people were happy to spend time together. Shanipiap, her faced still marked by her husband's blows, was trembling when Hélène had opened the door for her. The young Innu woman was nervously holding her round belly but had agreed to sit and drink a glass of water. Her hair framed her face with its well-drawn features and enormous eyes, which were as black as the North Shore's night sky.

Hélène had moved closer to Shanipiap and asked if everything was all right. That's all it had taken to make the expectant mother burst into tears. She had admitted that her life was sad and held no future, that she was sick and tired of it. Then Shanipiap had mustered her courage and whispered, "Tell me, Hélène, I know you're good with children, your house is always full of them... Would you adopt my baby, it's due in January?"

Hélène had been startled and replied in an uncertain tone. "Are you sure, Shanipiap? Maybe you're just going through a rough patch... Aren't you afraid you'll regret your decision later?"

Shanipiap had angrily shaken her head.

"No. I know I want to leave this godforsaken place where people treat me like a fool. They all know my husband beats me but no one does anything, not even the damn priest... I need to start over somewhere else... Believe me, Hélène, my baby will be happy with you, I know it, I had a dream about it!"

Pensive, Hélène had carefully observed the young Innu woman. She herself was married to a man who loved her dearly, but they had never been able to have children of their own and so had adopted three. She had told herself that one last little one would be worth the risk.

She had smiled and hugged Shanipiap, gently telling her that she would accept the offer.

Even today, 40 years later, Hélène had no regrets when she looked at her daughter. She knew that her youngest had not grown up in an easy world. Despite the prejudice that they had both endured, or perhaps because of it, a powerful bond united the two women.

Prejudice often came in the form of remarks that were innocent on the surface. How many times had the young mother been asked if she'd adopted a little Vietnamese girl? There were the interested looks of the neighbour lady or strangers that turned to disappointment when she mentioned her baby's origins. She still angrily remembered the day the village priest came to see her to deliver a reproachful sermon. He did not like seeing the little girl being raised by this somewhat rebellious family in his parish. He had commented on the morality of the two mothers and on his concern that the child be raised among Christians.

Hélène was aware that her country had a long way to go before it would acknowledge the past wrongs committed against her daughter's people and Canada's other Indigenous peoples. Anish's adoptive grandfather had been an Indian agent – a term that still provoked hostility among Indigenous people when they heard it. But not with Anish, who often told her friends about her grandfather. She latched onto the slightest positive examples that bore witness to the bridges built between Quebeckers and Indigenous peoples.

Hélène asked Anish if they could go back home. She wanted to be somewhere peaceful because the news she had to share with her daughter would not be easy to hear. Anish went to get the car and drove up to the store's exit. Her mother climbed in slowly, each movement causing her pain.

Hélène's house was sunlit, filled with flowers and watercolour paintings. It was furnished with the basics, and family photos hung on the walls. Hélène went to prepare herself some tea and asked Anish to come join her in the living room. She took her daughter's hand again to feel its warmth.

"Darling, I'm so happy to be spending time with you..."

Anish was paying close attention because her mother's voice had put her on her guard. Hélène never spoke to her with such sadness in her voice.

"Yes, Mom, what is it? You're scaring me..."

Hélène gathered her courage and began to speak. "Sweetie, my cancer is back. It's malignant...and...I've made my decision. I'm not going to have any chemo...and before you interrupt me, I'm telling you right away, my heart wouldn't survive the treatment."

Anish stopped breathing. She knew that one day she would have to face this ordeal. Panic engulfed her. That unbearable feeling of being abandoned.

Hélène went to her daughter and held her in her arms. Time was running out now. She had always worried about her daughter and wondered how she would manage once she was gone. Anish had been deeply affected by her origins as an Innu adopted by a white family, and it showed in the way she isolated herself. Hélène had noticed that her daughter studied the people, the situation, and the place before doing anything whatsoever. As if she were scouting the territory before beginning to explore it.

Anish remained silent. She couldn't share with her beloved mother the morbid thoughts running through her mind. She saw no future without her mother.

A woman walks along the shore; on her arm, a scar. The low tide emits a salty perfume carried by a gentle breeze. On her chest, a locket with two photographs, a man and a woman whose colour does not match her own. She chose to go on living, despite the unspeakable pain. Her soul is older now. Anish thinks that she will consider herself healed when she no longer regrets that she is still alive.

NASHTASH IN THE BIG CITY

JOSÉPHINE BACON
Innu from Betsiamites

According to the calendar, it was the second day of the month. Nashtash woke up, suffering badly from the night before. Stuff was lying all over the house – cases of beer, bottles on the table, shards of glass on the floor. The whole mess to clean up, and her boyfriend was still asleep. This time, she felt that she could not go through it again. The situation just kept repeating itself, every two months. Nothing ever changed.

Fortunately, it was sunny outside and the weather was gorgeous. She enjoyed this temperature, but she decided to go back inside to start picking up and putting away. Deep down, she wasn't happy, even though her laughter could be heard all the way down the street last night.

A nice shower will do the trick, she thought. Under the spray of water, she reviewed her life. *My grandparents are gone, so why stay when we've lost the teachings, forgotten our identity and changed our values? The grass has grown high along the portage route that dates back to the nomadic times of my ancestors. The river no longer speaks to me. The bottle has replaced the game we hunted when I was a child.*

Nashtash was Innu and always spoke her own language. She had a wild beauty and her black hair fell all the way down her back; she was tall in comparison to other young women her age and had a talent for dressing well. She was often told that she could have been a model.

This morning was not the first time that she had felt so uneasy, that she wondered what tomorrow would bring. From the corner of her eye, she spotted a knapsack. She took it as a sign and decided to pack up and leave. Route 138 might just lead her to another life.

The first car stopped and, what luck, it was a woman at the wheel! She was going to Sainte-Anne-de-Beaupré, another sign, thought Nashtash: the Innu like that town a lot. "A little prayer would be welcome," she told herself. Then she was on the shoulder of Route 138 once more.

A second car stopped, its driver a man with the air of a benefactor. She was not afraid, she was never afraid of human beings. A few hours later, they reached Montreal. Her benefactor drove her to the centre of town.

She saw young people wearing unconventional clothing; they seemed bizarre, but she was undaunted. One of them noticed her and came over to talk. She hit it off with them. They lived freely, as was their choice. She decided to adopt their lifestyle. She enjoyed washing windshields for a few dollars, which meant she could eat and find places to sleep.

Days passed. Nashtash seemed content with this life. She made friends who took care of her. They shared everything equally, which reminded her of her people's ancient traditions. She was in the right place, she was sure of it. She'd found meaning in her daily life.

One afternoon, as she was busy cleaning the windshield of a luxury car, the driver – a handsome man with ebony skin – handed her a twenty-dollar bill. She couldn't believe it. She thanked him and he smiled back at her.

She hoped to see him again. A few days passed and he kept coming back, always showing the same generosity, until one day he invited her to join him for a good meal at a restaurant he visited regularly. She could not accept – how would she look without the proper clothes to wear?

He told her that she had nothing to fear, he'd buy her the appropriate outfit for this sort of place, a wonderful evening lay ahead. In her dream that night, the man on her arm was a gentleman.

Nashtash was happy at last. She had left her friends to live with her ebony man. Every so often, she remembered what her life had been like back in her community. She missed it, of course, but this was the high life. He totally spoiled her and refused her nothing; he was there for her. She knew that she was in love, and so did he.

One day, her man admitted that he owed someone a large sum of money. She was deeply troubled. "I'll get a job to help you," she offered. She would do anything for him. But what? She hadn't learned a trade, did not have an education… That night, he suggested they go to a place he'd never taken her to before. She willingly agreed.

A dark place, mellow music, an empty stage. The girls were scantily dressed, they knew their man well. Music started to play, a girl appeared and began to dance. Her body moved in time to the music. Nashtash suddenly wanted to be somewhere else. Her memory took her back to her roots: it was the first of the month. She knew that this place was not for her anymore. For her, there would be no tomorrow.

Route 138 isn't too far from here, she thought. She had understood. She stood and told the man that she was going to freshen up. Once in the bathroom, she climbed onto the toilet bowl and out the window to the street below. She fled in the direction of the Jacques-Cartier Bridge. The road ahead would be long, but the river was there to guide her.

She travelled all night. When she finally arrived, it was sunny outside and the weather was gorgeous. She heard the laughter of her friends. They were thrilled to see her again, they had missed her. This time, the second day of the month fell on a Saturday. They told her that two bands would be playing music at the Grand Bar that night. They wanted her to join them there.

She entered her house. She was surprised to see that everything was where it belonged. Her boyfriend was there. He had stopped everything when she left and no longer drank.

"There'll be a sweat lodge, too," he told her.

THE AUTHORS

Michel Jean is an Innu writer, news anchor, and investigative journalist. After completing a Master's in History, he worked at Radio-Canada and, since 2005, at TVA. He has published eight critically acclaimed books and is the director of this collection of short stories.

Natasha Kanapé Fontaine is an Innu poet, spoken word artist, painter, actor, and Aboriginal rights activist from Pessamit. Mémoire d'encrier has published a number of her works including *N'entre pas dans mon âme avec tes chaussures* (Prix de poésie de la Société des Écrivains francophones d'Amérique 2013), *Manifeste Assi* (2014) and *Bleuets et abricots* (2016). *Kuei, je te salue* (Écosociété, 2016), a dialogue with Deni Ellis Béchard that has been translated into English as *Kuei, My Friend*, begins a conversation about racism and reconciliation.

Melissa Mollen Dupuis is Innu from Ekuanitshit in Quebec's North Shore region. She has worked for over 15 years with Native Montreal and the First Nations Garden, showing and sharing her culture's richness to the Montreal community. She explores contemporary ways to do so, using visual arts, video, performance and storytelling to communicate First Nations' culture. An actor in several Aboriginal television series, she is also involved in the Aboriginal cultural community with Réseau pour la stratégie urbaine de la communauté autochtone in Montreal, Wapikoni Mobile and Idle No More QC. In 2017, she was honoured with Amnesty International's Ambassador of Conscience Award.

Louis-Karl Picard-Sioui, native of Wendake, is an historian, anthropologist, writer, poet, and visual arts curator. He prefers not to be categorized, defining himself first and foremost as a creator. Picard-Sioui uses his writings to reinterpret the symbols and values of his people. His poetry has been circulated in periodicals, in exhibitions, on the Internet, and recited in Canada and abroad. It has been included in poetry collections and has even been adapted for an animated film. "Hannibalo-God-Mozilla Against the Great Cosmic Void" is his first published short story. His first collection of short stories, *Chroniques de Kitchike*, was published by Éditions Hannenorak in 2016.

Virginia Pésémapéo Bordeleau was born in Abitibi. She is a multidisciplinary artist of Cree and Métis heritage. A well-known painter in Quebec and abroad, she has exhibited her work in France, Mexico, and Denmark. In 2006, she won the excellence in creation award from the Conseil des arts et des lettres du Québec the Télé-Québec distinction in poetry. In 2012, she won the Prix littéraire de l'Abitibi-Témiscamingue. Mémoire d'encrier published her poetry collection, *De rouge et de blanc*, followed by the novel, *L'Amant du lac* (2013). Her novel, *Winter Child* (2017), was translated from the French by Susan Ouriou and Christelle Morelli.

Naomi Fontaine was born in Uashat, a small bay on the St. Lawrence River that is home to an Indian reserve and a landscape of tall pines. After completing her studies at the Université Laval, she returned to Uashat, where she had long dreamed of working as a teacher. Devoted to her people, she writes about who the Innu are and what their eyes have seen. Her first collection of poetic narratives, *Kuessipan*, was published in 2011 and translated into English by David Homel. Her second novel, *Manikanetish*, was published in 2017.

Alyssa Jérôme is a young Métis writer, actor, and singer from Sept-Îles, Quebec. At only 15, she published her first novel for young readers, *Le Rêve éveillé de Salma.* Two years later, she launched its sequel, *Le Rêve éveillé d'Amethyst.* During her adolescence, she discovered her passion for communications and pursued her studies in this field at Collège Jean-de-Brébeuf in Montreal.

Jean Sioui has published two novels for young readers, *Hannenorak* and *Hannenorak et le vent.* He is also the author of seven poetry collections. A member of the Wendat Nation, he writes in the spirit of First Nations. This culture, which is his ancestors', and thus his own by inheritance, is a source for his writings. His work is inspired by his involvement with budding Aboriginal authors and by his participation in numerous artistic events. He strongly supports the principles of respect, integrity and social justice, as well as the approach favouring the preservation of Huron-Wendat heritage and culture. Steeped in these values, he follows in his forebears' footsteps.

Maya Cousineau-Mollen, kindly nicknamed "little Innu pearl/gem" by her friend Michèle Audette, is a native of Mingan, on Quebec's Lower North Shore. Adopted by a French-Canadian family, Maya grew up between two worlds that once knew each other, no longer recognized each other, and are now relearning to reach out to each other. As Jack Monoloy's granddaughter, Maya was supported and encouraged to follow a career path toward writing. Her adoptive father, Pierre Cousineau, often told her to read, write, and complete her studies to gain her independence. Her adoptive mother, Gratia Maloney, was a fervent activist for the recognition of First Nations. Maya followed her family's advice and her first texts can be found in Maurizio Gatti's *Littérature amérindienne du Québec: Écrits de la langue française.* Her work has recently appeared in the periodicals *Moebius* and *Littoral*. She sees herself as a hybrid poet and French-Canadian Innu.

Joséphine Bacon is a poet, lyricist, and filmmaker. She has published four books, including two poetry collections. *Bâton à message/Tshissinuashitakana* was awarded the Prix des lecteurs du Marché de la poésie de Montreal in 2010. *Un thé dans la toundra/Nipishapui nete mushuat* (2013) was a finalist for Canada's Governor General's Literary Awards and for the Grand Prix du livre de Montreal. Bacon has received numerous distinctions, including an honorary doctorate from the Université Laval. She has made a significant contribution to the Innu community by documenting its language, culture, oral tradition, and history. She is regularly invited to international gatherings of Indigenous language writers and participates in numerous literary festivals and shows in Quebec and France.

TRANSLATOR'S NOTES

"I Burned All the Letters in My First Name"
  Miam nutau: (my) father
  Tshishe Manitu: the Great Spirit or the Great Mysterious
One, supernatural or spirit power associated with both good
and evil.

"Memekueshu"
  The Memekueshu are small rock spirits or "little people"
that live in caves. They are described as having narrow faces
and hairy bodies. They are friendly but shy of people and are
not usually dangerous, though they may cause trouble if they
are not treated with proper respect. (http://www.native-lan-
guages.org/innu-legends.htm)

"The Lakota Shaman"
  Charlie is variously referred to as the Sioux, the Lakota
and the Oglala. Settled in an area west of the Missouri River,
the Lakota are sometimes referred to as the Teton Sioux. This
group is divided into seven bands, one of which is the Oglala.
Charlie lives on the Pine Ridge Indian Reservation, which
serves the Oglala Sioux tribe in South Dakota.

"Where Are You?"
  Mashk: black bear
  Nishk: Canada goose
  Pekuakami: Lac Saint-Jean

"Mitatamun Means Regret"
  The author's use of Indian, American Indian or Native is
intentional. As the story progresses, the main character gains
experience and begins to use the terms Indigenous and Innu.

RECENT RELEASES
FROM EXILE EDITIONS

BAWAAJIGAN:
STORIES OF POWER

CO-EDITED BY NATHAN NIIGAN NOODIN ADLER
AND CHRISTINE MISKONOODINKWE SMITH

Bawaajigan – an Anishinaabemowin word for dream or vision – is a collection of short fiction by Indigenous writers from across Turtle Island. Ranging from gritty to gothic, hallucinatory to prophetic, the reader encounters ghosts haunting residential school hallways and ghosts looking on from the afterlife, bead-dreamers, talking eagles, Haudenosaunee wizards, giant snakes, sacred white buffalo calves, spider's silk, a burnt and blood-stained diary, wormholes, poppy-induced deliriums, Ouija boards, and imaginary friends among the many exhilarating forces that drive the Indigenous dream-worlds of today.

"This is, overall, a stunning collection of writing from Indigenous sources, stories with the power to transform character and reader alike...the high points are numerous and often dizzying in their force...

"This is an inspiring and demanding collection, and that is by design. The stories challenge readers on numerous levels: thematically, narratively, and linguistically...

"Anthologies like *Bawaajigan* can play a significant role in this process of education, removing passivity and distance from what might seem – to outsiders – like fantastic events, depicting both horrors and hope with an equal force and vitality." —*Quill & Quire*

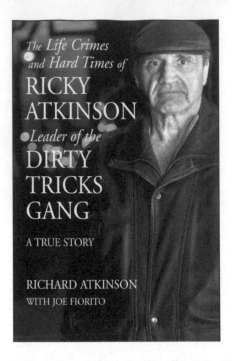

THE LIFE CRIMES AND HARD TIMES OF RICKY ATKINSON: LEADER OF THE DIRTY TRICKS GANG

RICHARD ATKINSON WITH JOE FIORITO

This is the life story of Ricky Atkinson, who grew up fast and hard in one of Toronto's toughest neighbourhoods during the social ferment of the 1960s, '70s, and '80s. His life was made all the more difficult coming from a black, white, and First Nations mixed family. Under his leadership, the gang eventually robbed more banks and pulled off so many jobs that it is unrivalled in Canadian history. Follow him from the mean streets to backroom plotting, to jail and back again, as he learns the hard lessons of leadership, courage and betrayal.

Today, after reconciling his past and life, he works to educate youth and people from all backgrounds about the no-win choice of being a criminal.

"Atkinson's memoir is as riveting as true crime gets… It is also a reckoning of the city's racist sins. [and he] makes the convincing connection between societal prejudice and crime in minority communities. It's a revelatory and fascinating story told from a rare perspective."
—*Publishers Weekly*, starred review

THE SILENCE

KAREN LEE WHITE

In *The Silence*, with the Yukon as a canvas, White engages in a deep empathy for characters, emergent Indigenous identity, and discovery that employs dreams, spirits, songs, and journals as foundations for dialogue between cultures, immersing the reader in a transitional world of embattled ethos and mythos. Her first novel is a *cri de coeur* that lives alongside Smart's *By Grand Central Station I Sat Down and Wept* and Kogawa's *Obasan*.

Karen Lee White holds the torch brightly as a new and powerful voice, her style and sensibility encompassing the traditional and the contemporary.

Includes (on the inside cover) a CD of the author/songwriter/musician's original music.

COYOTE CITY / BIG BUCK CITY
TWO PLAYS

DANIEL DAVID MOSES

A respected First Nations playwright and Governor General's Award finalist, Daniel David Moses is known for using storytelling and theatrical conventions to explore the consequences of the collision between Indigenous and non-Indigenous cultures. *Coyote City* and *Big Buck City* are the first two in his series of four City Plays that track the journey of one particular Native family between a world of Native spiritual traditions and the materialist urban landscape in which we all attempt to survive.

"*Coyote City*...in performance clearly would become a poem in its entirety... I've read nothing that conveys so powerfully how Canada and the future look to young Native men and women who choose the company of their own dead in preference to life in a society with no role or place for them. It's not just the best Canadian play I've read this year but the best in several years." —*Globe and Mail*

"While he offers plenty of pratfalls and broad caricatures, Moses ultimately aims for something darker, more complex, something magical. *Big Buck City* is a strangely powerful, disturbing piece of work...life and death and money and magic swirl around each other...an amusing but familiar farce [turns] into something more powerful and more difficult to pin down." —*Globe and Mail*

YO! WIKSAS?
HI! HOW ARE YOU?
AN ILLUSTRATED CONVERSATION WITH THE INVISIBLE GIRL SIRI

Rande Cook   Linda Rogers

YO! WIKSAS? / HI! HOW ARE YOU?
ART: RANDE COOK   TEXT: LINDA ROGERS

"Squirrel Nation and discerning kids everywhere will be delighted with this fun, fast-paced, and rollicking collection of poems by Linda Rogers, accompanied by silk screen images by Chief Rande Cook. *Yo! Wiksas?* is an innovative fusion of Kwakwaka'wakw art, Kwak'wala terms, and delightful English-language verse." —Richard Mackie, Editor, *The Ormsby Review*

Illustrated conversations are the Indigenous way of showing rather than telling, and these conversations between Isla and Ethan – son and daughter of Chief Rande Ola K'alapa (Cook), a much loved artist of mixed European and Indigenous decent – and their invisible friend Siri touch on bullying, environmental protection, and inclusivity – all very important topics for children. Isabel Rogers, also a kid, is part of the storytelling process.

We want this book to be a bridge, a route to one important thing: kindness… This book will also be a useful classroom adjunct to interpersonal relationships and a key to opening the potential for student narratives.